BULLETS

An Autumn Jade Mystery

BY
STEVE WHAN

I wish I was in China too, enjoy the story!
Steve

Autumn Jade Publishing
Vancouver

BULLETS ON THE BUND
Autumn Jade Publishing

ISBN 0-9688198-0-X

Published in Canada by Autumn Jade Publishing, Vancouver.
http://www.autumnjade.com

Printed in Canada

Cover Art by Trevor Lai

If I keep a green bough in my heart, the singing bird will come. - Chinese Proverb

This book is dedicated to my very own singing birds, Samantha Qiu Yu and Virginie Xiu Qian.

Map of Old Shanghai
(circa 1932)

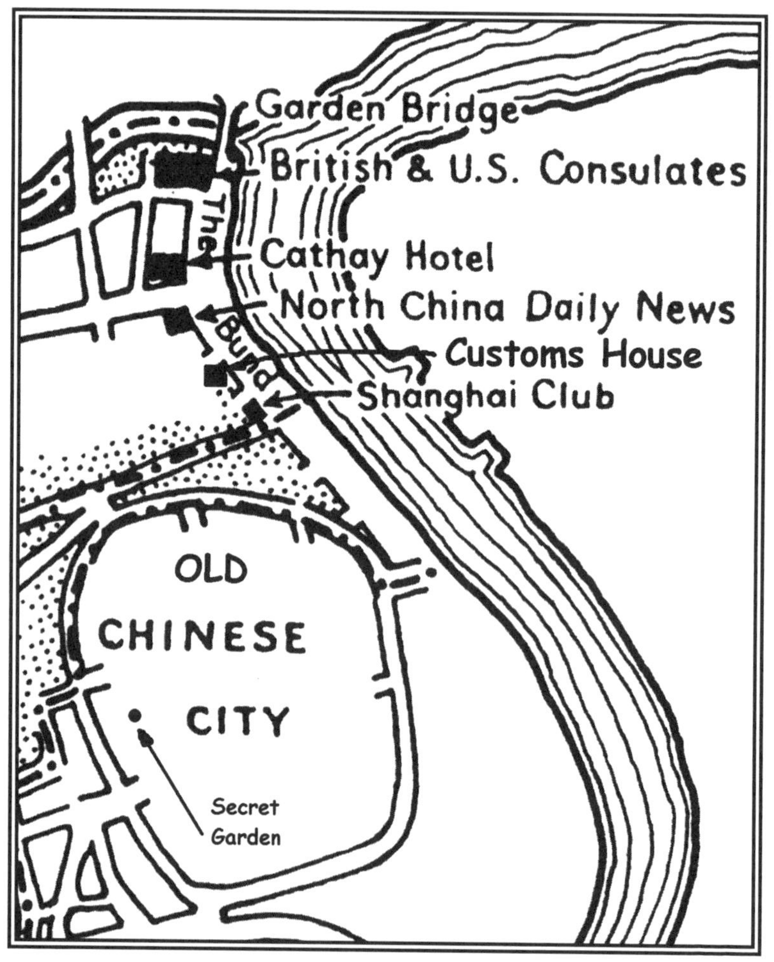

秋玉

1

Mrs. Pratt was standing at the side of the classroom, next to the huge picture window that overlooked the manicured lawn and the ocean beyond. Sunbathed in all its glory, the bright blue water looked entirely too inviting. The red maple leaf on the school's flag blew gently back and forth in the warm summer breeze.

"Now class, I know this is the last day of school but I wanted to do a short review of the material we've covered this year. As you recall, Canada was founded by..."

I looked over to see what Adam was doing. He was bending down to pick up a note lying at his feet. Vanessa, who was sitting on the opposite side of Adam, had a big smile on her suntanned face.

"Can anyone tell me who the first Prime Minister of Canada was?" asked Mrs. Pratt. "Adam, how about you?"

"Oh. I, err, excuse me Mrs. Pratt, what did you say?" Adam was obviously trying to buy some time.

"Sir John A. Macdonald," I said under my breath to him.

"What was that...?" he whispered back. "Uh, Johnny Mackenzie King," Adam quickly answered.

Poor Adam, he's my best friend but you could tell he hadn't been paying attention. Vanessa, with her long blond hair and designer clothes, must have really distracted him. What had she written, I wondered?

"John A. Macdonald," I called out, glaring at Adam.

"Thank-you Autumn," Mrs. Pratt said and continued on with her lecture.

I'm pretty good at Canadian history, but I would have preferred to hear about Shanghai in the 1930s. Over seventy years ago Shanghai had been called a city of mystery and intrigue, the Paris of the Orient. It was also the city where I had been abandoned when I was only one day old. I pulled out my notebook and my favourite pen. I'd recently been having a pretty vivid dream about old Shanghai and I wanted to write it down instead of listening to Mrs. Pratt's dreary monologue...

* * *

The early morning mist rolled gently off of the Whangpoo River and up onto The Bund, the main street of Shanghai's International Settlement. Ming found it amazing that clean, white mist could come off a river that was so yellow and filthy. People said that if you watched long enough, you would eventually see a body floating by.

There was a constant, bewildering sound of music in the air: the carrier coolies chanting to lighten their heavy loads and regulate their breathing, the subdued singing of men and women poling their sampans across the river. But Ming had no song in her heart today.

Liang Ming had come to Shanghai with several other women from her village. They had bananas, small and green, and ripe pomelos to sell at the market. Ming had another reason to be in the city. She carried a tiny, hidden bundle that she held close to her breast. The baby girl was only a day old. Ming hadn't thought she could feel so much love for such a little creature. Yet she had fed the infant with the milk of her body, and she felt the bond strengthen with every beat of her daughter's heart.

She could still remember the marriage ceremony ten months earlier. The Chen clan had consulted fortune-tellers for months in order to find a bride who would produce a boy for their eldest son. She had been the girl they had chosen. She had never been so happy as she was on her wedding day.

The marriage feast had been lavish and all the customs had been followed. She had been fetched from her parent's home, dressed in the finest red and gold cloth, her hair entwined with pearls and jade, bracelets on her arms and rings on each tiny finger. There were kowtows made to the images of the ancestors and five pigs were killed for the banquet. The guests ate glutinous rice cakes in abundance and the rice wine flowed. Everyone seemed to be already celebrating the birth of a new baby boy.

Ming's new husband and his family were most gentle with the new bride. The birth of a baby boy was the highest priority and she was told not to go into the fields or labour too hard.

Soon after the marriage, the pulse of a new life was beating through Ming's veins. It was the time for praying. All the women of the village lit candles and incense and on bent knees chanted prayers to Kwan-Yin, Goddess of Compassion, for the blessing of a son. The months passed quickly and soon it was time for the birth.

With her husband at her side and family members waiting nearby, the birth of the new baby went smoothly. Ming was unprepared for the elation she felt, the exhilaration of having carried a perfectly beautiful and healthy child to term. Even the dreary hut, the cold bed, and the impersonal midwife couldn't dim her happiness. Ming looked closely at the new baby, tracing the tiny ears, delicate nose, and smiling mouth with her finger. She had created a child, a real child. Life was beginning for a new person, separate and marvelous.

Perhaps the fortune had been poorly told, or perhaps she had encountered a peach ghost during her pregnancy. The nightmare began when her husband's mother entered the room and saw the naked child.

"How could you do this to us! It is a girl baby, we have no need for girls, she will have to be killed," her husband's Honourable Mother had shouted at her.

Her husband's younger brother threatened to beat the luckless soothsayer and also to beat Ming.

Old Auntie said, "Send Liang Ming back to her own family, she has brought us much disgrace."

Other Chen family clan members spoke of revenge as well. Through it all, her husband refused to look at his wife or the infant.

Then, quietly, the family resolved the problem between themselves.

"We will say that the baby disappeared during the night, taken away by the same ghosts who entered Ming and robbed her of the boy that was hers by right." Everyone agreed.

Ming was told to leave for Shanghai in the early hours of the morning with the other family members who were going to sell their fruit. She was to abandon the baby girl somewhere along the way. Death would be swift for a child left out in the open. With the whole family against her and with her husband refusing to even look at her, Ming had no choice but to agree.

Before Ming had traveled very far though, she had changed her mind. She had decided to disobey the family and when the time came she only pretended to leave her baby in a farmer's rice field. Frightened and desperate, she was now in the city with her daughter still tucked away under her clothing, hidden from the others. She had resolved to abandon her baby somewhere public enough that she would be quickly found, but private enough that no one would see Ming do it. Now that Ming was in Shanghai, she realized it might not be so easy.

Ming knew that only a foreigner or wealthy Chinese might save her child. But the British Consulate had guards at the gate and the foreign hotels were too crowded. She was scared sick. Her heart was beating too fast and there was a huge knot in her belly. She was worried now that her trembling might wake the child and then she would be caught.

There were tales about a place with a 'baby-drawer', a small wooden panel in a high brick wall where the child could be left. Chinese amahs under the supervision of Roman Catholic nuns raised the children. Ming didn't know where this building was and she didn't have the time to look for it.

Ahead of her, Ming could see a tall building with an enormous clock on the tower. The sign said Customs House and there were foreigners of all kinds in sight. Large packing crates and stacks of burlap-wrapped bundles provided cover, yet would soon be moved to their exotic destinations. This looked like it might be the place. It had to be the place. They were almost at the market and she was running out of time.

"I have to stop for a moment," Ming said to the others. "I will catch up."

"Are you okay?" asked her sister-in-law Chen Hua. "I can wait for you."

"No, keep on going, I will catch up shortly," Ming said, pointing at her bladder. Everyone nodded and they continued on without her.

Safely secluded, Ming whispered quietly to herself, "Ancestors, please give me strength."

"Mama's taking you out now, my precious child. Shh, shh, shh, don't cry. Don't cry now. I'm laying you softly on the ground where you will be found. Please don't hate me for this, I was given no choice."

Ming removed a pendant from around her neck. The teardrop-shaped piece of rare, purple jade had an intricate carving of an Imperial dragon on one side.

"This jade pendant comes from my mother and her mother before her. I place it around your neck hoping it brings you a happier life than mine."

Ming's bitter tears splashed onto her daughter's rosy cheek.

"Zaijian, my little one. Your mama will always love you, no matter where you are. Together we were whole, now I will be an empty shell. I promise that not a day will go by that I won't think about the daughter I had to give away."

It was too late to change her mind, she could hear footsteps approaching. Ming wiped her eyes and took several deep, sobbing breaths. Then she quickly turned and hurried to catch up with the others.

秋玉

2

Brrrringggg. The school bell snapped me back into reality. I finished writing down the first part of my dream and put my notebook into my backpack. Hooray! It was time for our summer vacation to start.

"All right class, pick up your things and walk out like the young ladies and gentleman that you are."

"Goodbye Mrs. Pratt," we all shouted.

"Have a great summer, children."

I met Adam at the end of the cloakroom and then we hurried to the front door of the school. "Free at last," he cried out as we flew down the steps into the schoolyard. "Yippee, we're free for the summer!"

Adam has been my best friend for practically forever. His parents adopted him from Atlanta, Georgia fifteen months before my parents adopted me from China. We'd grown up next door to each other and we were actually only a few months apart in age. My dad once said that our marriage was arranged right from the start. Hah! I knew that our parents couldn't do that. It was still possible in other parts of the world, but not here. Anyway, even though Adam probably was the hottest looking guy in school, we were just best friends.

We crowded through the school gates along with everyone else and then burst out into the glorious sunshine.

Out on the street, we met up with some of our friends.

Vanessa moved close to Adam. "Going to the lake this summer, Adam? That note was your invitation to stay at my parent's cottage, if you'd like." Vanessa had a crush on Adam, but Adam had never seemed interested in Vanessa except as a friend.

"Not sure yet, Vanessa. Autumn and I are still planning out our summer."

I said a quiet thank-you to myself and gave her my most charming smile.

I turned to Raj and Kayla. "You two going to the beach tomorrow?"

"Sure thing," they both chimed in. "What would a summer vacation be without spending our first official day at the beach?" Raj added.

"How about you, Autumn?" Kayla asked. "Any big plans for the summer?"

"My mom's been threatening to sign Watson and me up for a dog obedience class," I replied. "But I sure hope something better comes along. We'd better get going Adam, see you guys at the beach tomorrow!"

Adam and I headed down English Bluff toward 4th Avenue. We could see a big ferry heading out across Georgia Straight. The Gulf Islands were visible on the horizon, but it was too hazy today to see the American islands to the south.

"Wasn't that a great bicycle trip we did on Mayne Island last summer?" Adam sighed with a wistful tone to his voice.

"And getting Watson as a reward for finding Mr. Davis' prize race horse Dream Catcher was pretty amazing," I replied. "Let's hope this summer is just as exciting!"

4th Avenue dead-ended at Pebble Hill Park. Adam and I cut through the park, crossed over the top of the concrete water reservoir and came out by the parking lot. A hot pink Ms. Frosty truck was sitting in the nearest parking space with a line up of little kids waiting to be served.

Adam pointed at the truck. "Want to get something? I could really go for an ice cold fudgie-bar right about now."

"Sorry, I can't."

"How come?"

"I'm living in the poor house. My parents have started the process to go back to China and adopt another child. I'm doing my bit to economize. I can't believe they waited so long. I'm practically a teenager..."

"You're not a teenager yet!"

"Twelve is practically a teenager in my books. Anyway, Mr. Know-it-all, pretty soon I'll have a baby brother or sister to look after."

"Maybe they'll take you with them to China. Can you imagine seeing Shanghai for real?"

"Wow, you're right. Mom and Dad never mentioned it and I hadn't even thought to ask them. I bet they can't afford to have me on the trip so they didn't want to bring it up." We walked a few more steps. "You know, maybe a little brother or sister wouldn't be so bad after all."

"You should ask your Mom about the trip when you get home. Tell you what, I'll buy you an ice cream bar if you want."

"Thanks Adam, but I have to get in the habit of saving money. Especially if I have to convince my parents to take me to China! You should save yours too, and then you could loan me some of your money."

We were about to continue across the parking lot when a small, white dog with a big pack strapped on his back hobbled out from behind a car, right in front of us.

Adam's head snapped around. "Autumn, did you see that?"

"Yeah, he seems to be limping pretty badly. I wonder where the owner is? No one else seems to be around."

"Maybe he's lost. Let's see if we can catch him and look for an ID tag."

Adam started after the little dog. It was moving amazingly fast considering it had the backpack on and was limping. My legs may be shorter than Adam's but I quickly caught up to him.

"Where did he go?"

"I lost him."

"What do you mean you lost him? I thought all you black boys were natural athletes," I puffed.

"I got the wrong genes, I guess. Wait, there he is!"

The dog was almost into the trees.

"Come on, before we lose him again," I yelled back to Adam. "We've got to run faster!"

There was a big, forested area at the edge of the park. The little dog disappeared behind a green, leafy bush and headed into a stand of Douglas Fir trees. We both slowed down because the dog was nowhere in sight.

"Did you see where he went?" I called out.

"No, he just vanished into the trees."

"Let's split up. He can't have gotten too far."

We both tromped around in the bush for about five minutes, but the dog was gone. We met back in the park. Adam flopped down on the grass and I knelt down beside him, gasping for breath.

"Why would a dog be running through the park all on its own with a pack on its back?" I said between gulps of air.

"Pretty strange isn't it," Adam panted back. "We'll have to ask around and see if anyone else saw the dog."

"Sure, we can do that after dinner. I don't think he'll be coming back this way and it looks like he's gone for now."

We arrived at my house first. My parent's house is right in the middle of the block. It's an older two-storey house that's been completely fixed up. Adam and his parents live next door in another older house that was also renovated. A wonderful aroma wafted from the back of the house. I suddenly realized how hungry I was.

"See you later tonight, Adam?"

"Sure, it's summer vacation. We can stay up late and do anything we want!"

"Zaijian, Adam."

"Bye, Autumn!"

秋玉

3

Watson was lying on our big front porch staring right at me. You know, that spooky look that only a sheep-herding dog can give you, like their eyes are trying to burn a hole right through your body. His white fur with mottled brown and orange markings didn't really blend in with our blue-stained wood siding and white trim. It was difficult to take him too seriously.

"Can't you see I'm home, Watson? Aren't you going to get off your lazy butt and come down here and greet me?"

Watson wasn't actually lazy, but he only did what he wanted to do. He rolled over and looked away from me. Watson's tail gave him away, though. It was hitting the boards on the porch so hard you could hear him all the way out to the street.

"Aiya! Everyone else's dog runs over to meet them, why can't you?"

I ran up the steps and gave him an affectionate whack on the side of his head.

"You need an attitude adjustment, mister." He slowly got up and followed me into the house.

"I'm home," I shouted down the hallway.

"In my office, honey," came from the back of the house.

My mom has a home-based business. For as long as I can remember, she's worked from home designing and manufacturing her own line of children's clothes. Dad doesn't get home until after five o'clock, so Mom and I get to enjoy some private time together before he arrives. Last year after school she helped me create some of my own designs. I wanted to combine traditional Chinese styles with Western ideas and we came up with three very exciting outfits. The kids at school were sure surprised when I told them that my Mom and I had made them!

Dad works downtown doing computer stuff. Mom says he goes to work and plays all day; Dad says he gets to solve the problems that no one else can figure out. I guess they're both right, although I think it would be fun to work on computers all day and actually get paid for it.

"You look like you just ran a marathon," was the first thing Mom said.

"Adam saw this little dog with a backpack limping through the park. We tried to catch it, but we lost sight of it in the woods. We thought we'd ask around tonight and see if anyone knows whose dog it is."

"That's funny. Mrs. Chandler was just telling me yesterday that there have been some dognappings in the neighbourhood. She wanted to warn us because of Watson. You might want to see if she's home tonight. The number is on the fridge."

"Thanks Mom, I'll call her later. I'm glad she warned us, I'd sure hate to lose Watson."

Mom looked directly at Watson. "Speaking of which, I've signed you and Watson up for dog obedience classes at the Happy Puppy Obedience School all next week. Your first session is Monday morning at ten. I'll be dropping you off so you won't be late."

"Mom, how could you sign me up without even asking if it was okay?"

"Sorry, but I made the arrangements this morning and I can't cancel now."

"Do I have a choice?" I pretended to whine.

"You know our agreement, Autumn. We let you keep Watson because you promised to take obedience classes with him. You've postponed it long enough. He barely listens to you and he sure doesn't listen to your father and me. Watson's behaviour has to change this summer or we'll have to find him another home. With your new sister coming, we can't have a dog around that won't do what he's told."

"Wait a minute, did you say a sister? When did you decide on a girl and why didn't you tell me? What else haven't you told me about? Will I be going with you and Dad to China?"

"We can talk about all that later. Right now we're discussing you and Watson taking the obedience training."

"Okay, okay, we'll take the classes."

"Good. I'm sure you'll enjoy the course. The article I read on the Happy Puppy school said it was the best in town."

They'd have to be good to teach Watson anything. "Come on lazy bones, I guess we'd better go up to my room and start practicing."

As usual, my room was somewhere between a Good Housekeeping award winner and a nuclear test site. My bed and clothes were all neat and tidy, but my computer desk was straining under the weight of books and computer printouts. Parents can't complain if you meet them halfway, and I chose the half that stayed messy! On the wall behind my bed was a huge Chinese tapestry of a fierce red dragon fighting with a Mongolian tiger. In a glass cabinet beside the bed I kept all of my prized souvenirs from my parent's trip to China. Well, nearly all – the jade pendant they bought for me in Shanghai never left my neck.

I sat down in front of my computer. The framed newspaper article about Adam and me finding Mr. Davis' horse hung on the wall above my desk.

Watson curled up on his blanket and immediately fell asleep – so much for obedience training before dinner.

I grabbed a fistful of chips out of a bag wedged between two stacks of computer books. Dad had wired the whole house with our own network. Each of us had a super-fast Internet connection and our own email address. I was actually expecting a message from Dad, so I quickly launched my email program to see if anything new had come in.

I had five messages: one from Dad, three from the Sisters of China mailing list and a final one promising me 'up to $4000 a month' if I signed up for some stupid money-making scheme.

I deleted the last note and then opened the one from Dad.

My parents had purchased my jade pendant in a little out-of-the-way shop in Shanghai. They had been doing some sight-seeing before traveling to the orphanage. I was hoping to get some information about the pendant since we'd been told it might be quite valuable.

Subject: Jeweler's email address

Hi pumpkin, I found the email address for one of the big jewelry businesses in Shanghai. You should be able to send them the scanned picture of your jade pendant, plus the name of the shop where we bought it, and ask them if they have any information on the pendant.

See you in a bit...baba

"Yes!" I jumped out of my chair and startled Watson. I was usually pretty good at finding things on the 'net, but I'd been trying for days to track down someone in Shanghai. I'd finally given up and asked my dad if he could give it a try. I scribbled a reminder on my notepad to have him show me how he had found the jewelers.

I moved on to the first Sisters of China note. The SoC mailing list was a special email service for girls who had been adopted from China. Last time I checked there were over 4000 of us on the list. We all use our Chinese names. Mine is Qiu Yu, Qiu for Autumn and Yu for Jade.

From: Xue Lan <Snow Mist>

Subject: RE: boyfriends

Someone asked if twelve is too soon to have a boyfriend...

My mom and I had this big discussion about boyfriends and stuff last year. She said my age wasn't as important as how mature and responsible I could be. But, she didn't want to see me with some way older guy either – she said I wasn't ready for that yet. I agreed since I don't really know any older boys.

Anyway, if you can, you should talk to your mom about it. Even though your mom's older and stuff, she's probably been through it all with her own parents. Plus, if you try and be sneaky about it, your parents will find out and then good luck seeing your boyfriend.

And that's MHO...

MHO? I looked up at my email cheat sheet. Oh, right, my humble opinion. Luckily I didn't have that problem. All the boys at school, except for Adam of course, were pretty immature. Maybe junior high would be different. I deleted the note.

From: Ai Jie <Pure Love>

Subject: Language Lesson #1

Some people complained that they didn't receive my first Mandarin lesson, so I decided to re-send it to the list. You can find sound clips on my web site to hear how the phrases should be pronounced.

Basic Greetings:

Hello - Ni hao (pronounced knee how)

How are you - Ni hao ma

I am fine - Wo hen hao

Thank-you - Xiexie (pronounced sheh sheh)

Good-bye - Zaijian (pronounced zeye jen)

And try this on your parents:

Mama - Mother or

Baba - Father, for example, Ni hao ma, Baba

All pretty basic stuff. I pressed the delete key.

From: Li Xia <Beautiful Rosy Clouds in the Morning Light>

Subject: RE: Little Sisters

This has been a popular discussion thread for the past week. Seems like most parents who adopt from China think about going back for another child.

I remember just hating my little sister when my folks got back from China. Worse, I was supposed to share MY room with this tiny thing that cried and cried all night. My parents soon gave in though and moved Szu-chi into their room. It took a while, but it's kind of nice now having a little sister that looks up to me for advice on things.

Most parents don't wait almost twelve years before they adopt again!

I pushed aside the keyboard and reached for the phone. Guess I could try Mrs. Chandler now.

"Hello, Mrs. Chandler? It's Autumn from down the street."

"Hello, Autumn. How are you?"

"I'm fine, thanks. Mom said you were telling her about dogs going missing. Can Adam and I come over and talk to you about it tonight? We saw a little dog in the park..."

"I know, I saw the two of you chasing him."

"You saw him too? Wow. Would seven be okay?"

"Yes, that would be fine."

"Great, we'll see you then."

I quickly dialed Adam's number but I only got the answering machine.

"Adam, where are you? We're paying Mrs. Chandler a visit tonight. She might know something about the dog. Be ready by ten to seven. I'll fill you in on the way. Zaijian."

秋玉

4

Shanghai, 1927. This was going to be Qiu Yu's seventh Chinese New Year. The whole process for celebrating a New Year properly was very complicated, but Qiu was thinking that she had it mostly figured out. She played her role as the obedient daughter even if her heart wasn't always in it. Qiu turned to face Mama, sitting next to her in the taxi.

"The first day of the Lunar New Year is the welcoming of the gods of the heavens and earth," Qiu began. "We abstain from meat on the first day of the New Year to ensure a long and happy life. On the second day, we pray to our ancestors as well as to all the gods. We should be extra kind to dogs and feed them well because the second day is the birthday of all dogs. Then, sorry Mama, what comes next?"

"The third and fourth days are for sons-in-law to pay respect to their parents-in-law," Mama filled in.

"Okay, right. The fifth day is called Po Woo. On that day people stay home to welcome the God of Wealth. No one visits families and friends on the fifth day because it will bring both parties bad luck. On the sixth to the tenth day, we visit our relatives and friends. We also visit the temples to pray for good fortune and health.

"Correct. Please continue," Mama smiled.

"The seventh day of the New Year is the day for farmers to display their produce. The farmers make a drink from seven types of vegetables to celebrate the occasion. The seventh day is also considered the birthday of human beings. We eat noodles to promote longevity and raw fish for success. On the eighth day we have another family reunion dinner, and then at midnight we pray to Tian Gong, the God of Heaven. On the ninth day we make offerings to the Jade Emperor, hey, just like my pendant!"

"Very good, Qiu, and finally," Mama prompted.

"The tenth through the twelfth are days that friends and relatives are invited for dinner. After so much rich food, we have simple rice congee and mustard greens on the thirteenth day to cleanse our systems. The fourteenth day we prepare to celebrate the Lantern Festival that is to be held on the fifteenth night. On New Year's Day, we eat a special meal. The Lotus seeds signify having many male offspring. Ginkgo nuts represents silver ingots. Black moss seaweed is for exceeding in wealth. Dried bean curd represents fulfillment of wealth and happiness. Bamboo shoots is a term that sounds like 'wishing that everything would be well.'"

"How do we prepare these special foods?"

"We leave the fish whole, to represent togetherness and abundance. Chickens are for prosperity. The chicken must be presented with a head, tail and feet to symbolize completeness. Noodles should be uncut, to represent long life. We never serve fresh bean curd because it is white, which signifies death and misfortune. This is unlucky for New Year."

"Well done, Qiu Yu!" Mama said, clasping Qiu's small hands in hers. "Maybe next year we'll put you in charge of all the arrangements for our New Year celebrations."

"No thank-you, Mama. I'd prefer to eat the food and play with my friends."

The taxi stopped in front of a clean, brick house in one of the neighbourhoods reserved in Shanghai for well-off Chinese. Qiu's father worked as a comprador for one of the big British merchant companies. He was paid very handsomely for acting as the middleman between the Chinese and the foreigners. Mama paid the driver and they stepped through the gate into the front courtyard.

The gardener was busy planting a row of plum blossom plants.

"Lucky is the home with a plant that blooms on New Year's Day, for that foretells a year of prosperity," he called out.

"They are very beautiful, Mr. Ho," Qiu responded.

The living room was decorated with vases of pretty blossoms, platters of oranges and tangerines as symbols for abundant happiness, and a candy tray with eight varieties of dried sweet fruit.

"What do the items in the candy tray represent?" Mama asked, continuing Qiu's test.

"Candied melons are for growth and good health, red melon seed to symbolize joy, happiness, truth and sincerity, lychee nuts for strong family relationships. Kumquat means prosperity because they are gold coloured, coconut for togetherness, peanuts represent long life, longnan for many good sons and lotus seeds for many children," Qiu recited from memory.

On the walls and doors were poetic couplets, happy wishes written on red paper. "May you enjoy continuous good health" and "May the Star of Happiness, the Star of Wealth and the Star of Longevity shine on you" were two of Qiu's favourites.

The houseboy was busy doing a final cleanup of the house.

Sweeping could not be done on New Year's Day for fear that good fortune would be swept away.

Qiu could hear her father talking in heated tones to someone in his study. Mama went to see how arrangements in the kitchen were progressing. Qiu quietly tiptoed over to the study door and put her eye up to the keyhole to see what was happening.

There was an angry looking Japanese man in a formal gray kimono facing Qiu's father. "So you refuse our generous offer?"

"Your offer is not welcome here," replied her father. "Now kindly leave my house."

"You will live to regret this! Our business today is concluded, but you have been warned."

Qiu jumped from back the door and pretended to be re-arranging flowers in a vase. The Japanese man stormed by her and left without another word. Qiu's father put a gentle hand on her shoulder.

"How much of that did you hear?"

"Enough to be scared, Baba."

"Please come into my study for a minute, Qiu Yu."

Qiu sat in the comfy armchair across from her father's desk.

"You are my only child, Qiu Yu. Since I found you abandoned on the wharf seven years ago you've been both a daughter and a son to me. There are dark days ahead for China and I want you to be prepared for whatever may come. The responsibilities of the family business ventures may fall to you sooner than I would like."

"What do you mean, Baba? What did that man say to you?"

"The Japanese want all of Asia for themselves, starting with China."

"Isn't that what the other foreigners want as well?" Qiu interrupted.

"The British, the French and all the rest have been limited to the Treaty Ports like Shanghai and Canton. We know how to deal with them and, except for a handful of foreign missionaries working in the countryside, they leave most of China alone and unharmed."

Qiu's father sighed. "The Japanese are not like that and now I'm worried. Mr. Uzuki actually had the audacity to threaten me. They need people on the inside to sabotage the foreigners' operations. I politely refused, but Mr. Uzuki said that 'no' was not an acceptable answer. It's a bad omen that he should talk like that just before the New Year. It is not a good sign at all."

"Couldn't we travel abroad again, like we did when I was younger? We could leave China until things are better."

"Our traveling days are over. Your mother and I love this country and we're here to stay. However, if anything bad should happen, I've made arrangements for your Auntie Shu-Shu to become your guardian."

Qiu scrunched up her face. "Not her! You can't be serious."

"Your Auntie Shu-Shu is my only living relative. I wouldn't trust your upbringing to anyone other than a close family member."

"But..."

"Now don't you worry, it's just a precaution. I'm sure nothing will come of all this."

Qiu put on her best look of disapproval. "That's easy for you to say, you won't be stuck living with her."

"Now, now, Qiu Yu. Your mother and I are going out tonight and Auntie Shu-Shu will be here soon to look after you. Please try to be respectful and above all, behave yourself."

"Yes, Baba."

Auntie Shu-Shu arrived promptly at six o'clock. Qiu Yu's parents left and the hours slowly dragged by. Auntie Shu-Shu treated Qiu more like a servant girl than her brother's number one daughter.

"Qiu Yu," Auntie called out, "more tea please, and bring me more of those delicious sweet meats."

As Qiu poured the tea, a messenger coolie appeared in the front courtyard. The note was quickly relayed to Auntie Shu-Shu. She read the note and fainted. Qiu pulled the note from her Auntie's limp hand.

'Mother and father killed in front of Cathay Hotel. Please advise...Chen Po-Li.'

Losing parents twice in such a short lifetime was too much. Qiu Yu's world went black as she also collapsed to the floor.

秋玉

5

"Autumn, your dinner's ready," Mom shouted from downstairs.

"Okay!" I put down my notebook and headed out the door.

Mom always cooked a special meal on Friday nights. After two big helpings of lasagna and garlic bread, I excused myself from the table and ran next door to Adam's house.

"Adam, are you ready to go?"

"Sure thing!"

It was one of those wonderful summer evenings when the whole neighbourhood comes alive. Nearly everyone was out mowing their lawn, puttering in the garden, or walking their dog. It was a great opportunity to ask people if they knew anything about the dog we had seen. Mr. Clancy was trimming a hedge and next door to him, Mrs. Bothra was watering her prize roses.

"Hi, Mr. Clancy," Adam waved. "We saw an injured dog in the park today and it didn't have an owner. Do you know anyone who might be missing a small white dog?"

"Sorry, it doesn't ring a bell."

"Hello, Mrs. Bothra," I said.

"Hello, children, beautiful evening, isn't it."

"Yes it is. We're asking everyone if they've seen a little white dog, or know someone who's missing one."

"I haven't heard of anything, but have you thought of talking to Mrs. Chandler?" she asked. "She knows everything that goes on around here. If I were you, that's where I'd go."

"That's where we're heading now. Thanks."

Mrs. Chandler lived by herself in a small one-storey house at the end of the block. Even though she was now 68 years old, she still maintained the house and yard herself. Her husband was killed in a forest accident in the 1950's, so she'd had to raise their two kids all on her own. I'd once heard someone say that you couldn't name any job that she hadn't done at some point in her life. Mom calls her one amazing lady.

We turned up her driveway and used the sidewalk to reach the front door. Adam raised his right hand and gave it two polite but solid knocks with his knuckles.

"Coming."

A tall, slender woman with strawberry blonde hair piled high on her head opened the door.

"Oh, hello Autumn, hello Adam," Mrs. Chandler said. "You're right on time. Let's go through the house and sit out on the back patio. I've got some ice cold, home-made lemonade if you kids still drink that kind of thing."

"Sure we do, thanks," Adam said.

"You two make yourselves comfortable and I'll be out in a jiffy with the lemonade."

"What's a jiffy?" Adam whispered.

"Adam, be nice! I think it means she'll be right back."

There were four white lawn chairs and an umbrella-covered table sitting on the red brick patio. I sank into the chair cushions and looked around.

"What an incredible garden," I said. "It has a real Oriental feel to it."

"Must take an awful lot of work," Adam agreed, staring at the carefully manicured lawn.

"Some people spend a lifetime perfecting their garden," I replied.

Mrs. Chandler arrived with a cool pitcher of lemonade, three glasses and a tray of homemade peanut butter cookies.

"That's right, Autumn. I've spent over fifteen years working on my garden. I'm glad you like it."

"It's very beautiful, Mrs. Chandler. Could I come over and help you work on it?"

"It would be a pleasure, Autumn. Now children, let's get down to business."

"We were hoping you can tell us something about the missing dogs," I said.

"And do you know who owns the white dog we were chasing?" Adam added. "The poor thing was limping and I'd sure like to find the owner."

"I'm afraid your little white dog isn't one of dogs I've heard about. There are at least four other dogs that I know of that have disappeared recently. Two black labs, one with white feet which is very unusual, a Jack Russell terrier and a brown and white Heinz 57."

"A what?" Adam asked.

"Sorry, Adam. A Heinz 57 is a dog that looks like it has many different breeds all mixed up in one. Anyway, one of the owners contacted the police and was told that they'd received quite a few calls lately about dogs that had gone missing. The police also told him that they wouldn't look for missing pets, so nothing could be done about his dog."

Adam's eyes went wide. "Has anyone seen the missing dogs?"

"A friend of mine called one night last week to say she'd just seen a big brown and white dog with a backpack running down the street. It had come running up from behind and nearly scared her to death. It matched the description of one of the four dogs."

"Hey," Adam said, "the one we saw had a backpack on, too."

"I know, and I find that very interesting. It normally takes a lot of training to get a dog to wear a pack of any kind. It's hard to imagine seeing two different dogs doing it."

"What do you mean?" I asked.

"I've owned many dogs in my life, but only one of them let me put a backpack on him. Bobby was his name. We were trying to get accepted for a Search and Rescue program. I had to pull out all the tricks I knew to get that backpack on him."

"What kind of tricks, Mrs. Chandler?" I asked. I told her all about Watson and the course we were going to take at the Happy Puppy Obedience School.

"To start with, all dogs are pack animals by nature. The head of the pack is called the alpha dog. To successfully train a dog, you have to establish that you're alpha dog and that they are beta dog."

"Just like the Latin alphabet," Adam said. "Alpha, beta, gamma, delta... and I can't remember the rest."

"Exactly. A dog's instinct to lead is associated with the act of going first in the pack, being alpha dog. When you let it precede you and other people through an outside door, for example, your dog instinctively accepts this as a sign of its dominance. Your dog needs consistent signals that people, especially you as alpha dog, are always the leaders. It is important that people always go first, even for something as simple as entering or leaving the house. If you have more than one dog, each of you has to know what your place in the pack is. But remember, you are always the alpha dog, and you have to put yourself first or they'll never listen to you."

Mrs. Chandler picked up the pitcher of lemonade and refilled everyone's glasses.

"The second thing is that most dogs will do everything they can to make you happy. Dogs have been bred for thousands of years to serve, so they have a built in desire to work really hard for us. The trick is to find a good reason for a dog to want to do something for you. For example, with the backpack, I started by putting Bobby's treats in it and carrying it with us on long walks. When he got used to the pack, and knew it was a source of the treats, I would strap it on him for short trips. Gradually we worked up to him carrying it all the time."

"Did you get into Search and Rescue?" Adam asked.

"No. Unfortunately for me, Bobby got lost during our big test. A dog can smell one hundred times better than people do, but I think Bobby's nose wasn't all that good. Dogs are supposed to remember a smell like humans remember a face, but it never worked that way for him. We ended up using the instructor's dog to find Bobby, and that was the end of our chance to help find lost hikers." Mrs. Chandler chuckled quietly to herself.

"This is great!" I said. "I should be taking notes. Watson needs all the help he can get, you know."

"Actually, Autumn, any good obedience school is teaching you, not your dog. You need to learn how to be alpha dog and what the commands and signals are to get Watson to obey you. You know, I recall reading about the Happy Puppy school when it opened. The local paper had an article about how the old owners had been bought out by an American company who paid a lot more for it than everyone thought it was worth."

"Whatever happened to Bobby?" Adam interrupted. I guess he wanted to know how the story turned out.

"Well, we ended up passing a pet therapy test and went on to visit with the residents of a local retirement home until Bobby finally died. Even though Bobby got lost all the time, he was sure good with people."

Mrs. Chandler stood up to stretch. "Well, I've talked long enough and it's starting to get dark. Besides that, I think you have a visitor hiding behind that planter, Autumn."

I jumped up to get a better view and there was Watson curled up on the lawn.

"What am I going to do with him? I told him to stay in our yard."

"I think you'll have to work especially hard at the obedience course," laughed Mrs. Chandler.

"Yes, I will. Thanks a lot for all the information and training tips."

"And the lemonade and cookies," Adam added.

"You're welcome. Goodnight, and come again anytime. Good luck finding the owner of the little white dog!"

"Let's go, Watson," I called out.

秋玉

6

Next morning at the beach, I told our friends about the big chase. Oddly enough, Kayla and her cousin Ben had both heard about dogs going missing, too.

"Do you know what the dogs looked like?" Adam asked. "Was either of them a small white dog like the one we chased?"

"I think our neighbour's dog was a German Shepherd cross of some sort," Kayla said.

Ben looked thoughtful for a minute. "And my friend's dog was a chocolate lab."

"Too bad," Adam said. "I'd really like to find out who owns the dog. I'm starting to feel very sorry for it."

"How are you going to find the owner?" Raj asked.

"And why did it have the backpack on?" Ben added.

Kayla said, "Are you sure it was really lost?"

Adam waved his hands at everyone. "Whoa, too many questions at once. I don't know if it was really lost, but it looked hurt and there was no owner around. We have no idea why it had the backpack on, and when we talked to a neighbour about it last night, she said that that was pretty unusual. I'd sure like to find the owner. Any ideas?"

"How about the S.P.C.A?"

"Or the police?"

"Classified Ads in the paper, the Missing Pets section."

Adam scribbled notes on a scrap of paper. "Those are all great suggestions, thanks."

"Well, I hope you find the owner soon," Kayla said.

"Yeah, me too," Ben added.

Vanessa had joined the group about halfway into the conversation. She moved close to Adam. "I'd be glad to help you look for the dog."

"Thanks for the offer, Vanessa. I'll let you know."

"Enough talk, you guys," Raj pleaded. "Let's go swimming!"

A little while later we were all relaxing on our beach towels, basking in the sunshine.

Vanessa had put her towel right next to Adam's. Her getting close to Adam was really starting to irritate me. I turned to look at Adam and whispered, "Are you still awake over there? Thanks for the offer, I'll let you know. Let her know what?"

No response. Either he was already asleep or he didn't want to talk about it. Two could play that game. I pulled out my Shanghai notebook...

* * *

Qiu Yu clapped her hands. "Three nines! Pay up, I win again!"

Lin the cook and Ju the houseboy both threw down their cards in disgust.

"Little Missee cheating again I think," Lin grumbled. "I bet your friends show you how."

"You two play so badly I don't need to cheat," Qiu retorted.

"One more hand?"

"No, time to work now," Ju said. "Your Auntie will be home soon, lots to do. Anyway, I got nothing left to bet with except the shirt on my back and Honourable Auntie would be very unhappy if I serve dinner without it."

"Spoil sport. We'll play again tomorrow?" Qiu asked sweetly.

"You bet, Missee," they both laughed.

Qiu Yu had now been living with Auntie Shu-Shu for nearly five years. The first few months had been the lowest point in Qiu's short but troubled life. Auntie Shu-Shu had handled all of the funeral arrangements after Qiu's parents' death. She had treated Qiu Yu like she was her own daughter during the period of mourning. However, as soon as she was legally Qiu's guardian and the trust fund was in her hands, Auntie sent Qiu to work in the kitchen along with the servants.

"While I'm in charge, you will do as I say," Auntie Shu-Shu had flatly stated.

"You can't do this!" Qiu protested.

Auntie slapped her several times and then sent a sobbing Qiu Yu off to the kitchen to start her new life. Qiu barely remembered the next four years. It was only during this past year that life had become bearable again. She had recently found two new friends, Amy and Soo-Lin. Without them, life would have been sheer misery.

Qiu Yu first met Amy at the Chocolate Shop, the only place you could get real American ice cream in all of Shanghai, and maybe even all of China. The Chocolate Shop jutted out into Nanking Road, across from Kelley & Walsh's Bookstore. Even Madam Sun Yat-sen would visit the Chocolate Shop when she wanted some ice cream!

One Friday afternoon, Qiu had gone to the Chocolate Shop to

pick up some strawberry ice cream for her Auntie. Amy was sitting with her dad at a small table by the window. There weren't many kids of their age in the International Settlement, so Amy came over to talk while Qiu waited for her order to be filled.

"Ni hao," she said. "My name is Amy. Would you like to join us?"

"Ni hao, I'm Qiu Yu. I would love to sit with you, but do you think it will be all right with your father?"

"Sure! Come on, I'll introduce you to him."

"Qiu Yu, this is my father. He works at the British Consulate. Dad, this is Qiu Yu."

Amy's father was a very tall man with silver hair. He put out his hand.

"A pleasure to meet you, Qiu Yu," he said in a beautiful baritone voice.

"Nice to meet you too, sir," Qiu replied.

Amy and Qiu hit it off right away. Amy's dad must have felt pretty left out, because he eventually excused himself. The girls kept talking and talking. It turned out that Amy and Qiu had both traveled all over the world and they couldn't believe the number of similar stories they shared.

Amy and Qiu Yu were the best of friends from that first day at the Chocolate Shop. It was a month later that they met Soo-Lin.

Soo-Lin was a Creek-Child. That meant her family lived on a boat in Soochow Creek. Amy and Qiu met Soo-Lin one afternoon while they were out exploring the city. The streets were crowded with trolleys, taxis, rickshaws and bicycles. It looked like an army of rickshaws had jammed up the intersection they were trying to cross. A big turbaned Sikh from the Punjab was cracking his truncheon to move the traffic. Amy and Qiu both saw Soo-Lin at the same time, trying to rescue her younger brother from the wheels of a rickshaw.

"Quick," Amy shouted, "we have to help her."

They dashed out into the traffic, dodging moving vehicles of every description. Somehow Amy made it through and snatched up Soo-Lin's brother before the wheel crushed him. Soo-Lin was so grateful that she offered to be their personal guide whenever they wanted to see more of the city.

"I can show you all sorts of exciting places," she had told them. "I even know of a secret garden where we can meet."

* * *

Adam reached over and gave me a gentle poke in the ribs. "Whatcha writing about?"

"Nothing much."

秋玉

7

Monday morning arrived and Mom dropped Watson and me off at the Happy Puppy Obedience School just before nine forty-five. 'Better to be early' was one of my mother's favourite sayings.

"Have fun, you two! I'll be back at eleven-thirty."

"Thanks Mom. We'll try and have a good time."

After Mom drove off, I knelt down, grabbed Watson by his ears and stared him directly in the eye.

"So here's the deal, Mr. Puppy. You're going to be a good boy and not embarrass me today. Okay?"

I took the lick on my nose as a yes.

We appeared to be the first to arrive. At the end of the parking lot a two-storey building had a large red "Happy Puppy Obedience School" neon sign on the roof. Mom had told me that the obedience class met in a room on the first floor. Behind the main building was a fenced off grassy area with all sorts of jumps, ramps, tunnels and stuff. Beside it was a long, low building that had "Kennel" in small letters on the awning over the door. I could hear dogs barking in the kennel. The whole place looked like a hobby farm that someone had converted into a dog school.

"Maybe I should leave you in the kennel until you graduate. What do you think of that?" I asked Watson.

I got another lick on my nose.

"Thanks, Watson. We may as well go inside."

I opened the door and waited for Watson to catch up. I went through first just like Mrs. Chandler had said. There was a woman with greasy brown hair sitting in the front office.

"Excuse me, which way to the obedience class?"

"At the end of the hall and on your left," Ms. Greasy Hair said without looking up from her glossy magazine.

"Thanks."

"Boy, Watson," I whispered as we walked down the hallway, "someone with worse manners than yours. Maybe she should be taking the course."

The meeting room was easy to spot: there was a big cardboard sign announcing the Obedience Level 1 course.

"Good morning," said a pretty, blonde woman standing in the middle of the room. "My name is Leslie and I'll be teaching the class. Come on in."

Sitting perfectly still beside Leslie was a black and white Border Collie.

"Sadie, stay," Leslie said very quietly and then walked over to us.

"And who do we have here?" she asked.

"This is Watson, and I'm Autumn."

"Nice to meet both of you. Can he shake a paw?"

"Sorry, he isn't very well trained. I guess that's why I'm here."

"That's okay, Autumn. I think you'll be nicely surprised by the difference in Watson by the time you both finish the course."

"I'll really see a change with just a week's training?"

"Believe me, you'll be amazed at the improvement."

The other students started arriving. Leslie welcomed each of them as they came through the door.

"Good morning, come on in."

Once everyone was in the room, Leslie went up to the front to start the class.

"This is the Happy Puppy Obedience Level One course. My name is Leslie, and this is my dog Sadie. I'll be your instructor this week. We'll all be heading out to the training area in a few minutes. Before we do though, I want to cover a few rules and give you an overview of what you'll be learning this week.

"To start with, this is work time for your dogs. We'll take some short breaks, but at no time should you allow the dogs to play together while in the class. It makes it too hard to keep their attention if they think they have a playmate nearby.

"Rule number two: there is equipment in the training area that you might be tempted to try – please don't. Your dog could easily get injured without proper knowledge of how to use the jumps, ramps and teeter-totters.

"Three, if your dog poops, please pick it up. There are bags available if you don't have any with you."

I looked over at Watson and hoped he could hold it.

"Four, please don't reward your dog with treats. It distracts the other dogs and we find that in the long run, a dog trained with praise instead of treats will listen better.

"And finally, number five: please don't wander outside of the fenced area. We don't want the people working in the kennel to be interrupted."

Leslie glanced down at her notes.

"Today we'll be covering sit, stay, and doing lots of heeling practice. Tomorrow we'll work on turning, stand and stand-stay. By the end of the week, I'm hoping all of your dogs will down-stay, come when called, and maybe even know a few tricks. Any questions?" Leslie paused. "Okay, everyone please say your dog's name followed by 'heel' and let's all go outside. Sadie, heel."

Once we were all outside, Leslie took Sadie over to the obstacle course.

"Before we begin, I want to show you what a highly trained dog can do. Sadie, go!"

Using only short whistles and hand signals, Leslie took her dog through the obstacle course. Sadie's feet hardly touched the ground as she flew over the jumps, traversed the ramps and ran through the hoops and tunnels. All of our jaws dropped open in amazement as we watched Sadie. She was through the course in no time at all.

"Unbelievable," said one of the students. "How long did it take you to teach her that?"

"We've been working at it for several months," Leslie replied. "It doesn't take long if the dog wants to learn and you know what you're doing."

Leslie put Sadie in a down-stay under the shade of a fruit tree and came back to the group.

"A dog respects and appreciates a firm master. We'll warm up by getting your dog to walk beside you. Once again, say your dog's name and then in a firm voice give the command 'heel.' Follow along in a big circle until you get back here."

We worked with the dogs for about half an hour and then Leslie called a break.

"Everyone take five minutes. Get your dogs some water and let them go to the bathroom if they need to."

I gave Watson a big hug.

"Good boy," I said, "you're doing so well today!"

After the break, Leslie showed us how to get a dog to sit on command.

"The best way to get your dog to sit," she began, "is to work with them when you're out for a walk together. If you stop and they sit on their own, reinforce it with a 'sit' command followed by lots of praise."

"What if we've never done that?" asked one of the students.

Leslie positioned Sadie at her side. "Then we do it the old-fashioned way. It's actually very simple. The verbal command is 'sit.' As with most commands, do not use your dog's name before giving the command. Only use your dog's name with commands that involve moving forward, like 'heel' or 'come.' Okay everyone, let's give it a try."

It was 11:30 before we knew it. Watson was completely exhausted.

"That's all for today," Leslie said. "Please let your dogs take it easy, they're going to be pretty tired. For homework tonight I want you to practice, but please, no more than ten minutes. I'll see you all tomorrow morning. Hope you enjoyed your first day."

Mom was waiting for us in the parking lot.

"How was the class, honey? Watson sure looks pooped."

"It was great Mom, and Watson was the best dog in the class. See, his tail is wagging he's so happy. I can hardly wait for tomorrow's session."

"I have your bag in the trunk. Do you want to go straight to the beach, or did you want to come home first? We still have some lasagna leftovers in the fridge."

"Actually Mom, could you drop me off at the library and then take Watson home? I want to get a book on dog obedience and look up some other things."

"You sure you don't want to have some lunch first?"

"I'll be fine, I had a big breakfast and I packed some snacks for the beach. Can I use your cell phone to call Adam and let him know?"

"Sure."

"Thanks, Mom."

Besides finding some dog obedience books, there were a couple of things I wanted to look up before we headed to the beach. I figured I should look up the Happy Puppy news item that Mrs. Chandler had talked about and we could also check for ads about missing dogs.

秋玉

8

It was going to be a little while before Adam made it to the library by bus. I decided to find the dog obedience books first and maybe hang out in the Asia collection until he showed up.

My favourite librarian, Wendy, was on duty at the front desk. Most people think librarians are all older women with gray hair tied up in a bun. Wendy is anything but that. She's young and she has this enormous mane of bright red hair. She always dresses in purple: blouse, pants, socks, shoes. I guess she likes the colour. I waved at Wendy and went over to see her.

Wendy offered me the chair next to her desk. "Hi Autumn! Here to get some books on Shanghai?"

"No, I'm looking for dog obedience books this time. Watson and I are taking a course and I want to learn more about it."

"Need any help?"

"Not for the dog books, but I might need your advice later on."

"I'm here all day. Just come and find me when you need a hand."

I said thanks and headed over to the computer terminals.

To find a book in the library I always do a title keyword search.

Doing an exact title match or subject search doesn't always show the books you want. Then I write down the main call numbers and go look in the stacks. I'd often found the perfect book that way even though it didn't show up in the search return.

I typed in 'dog', hit ENTER and then scrolled through looking for the call number for obedience books. 636.708 seemed to be the most common number. I wrote down the number using the pencil and scrap paper beside the terminal and went to find the books.

Hmmm, 635, 636. The 'Great Big Book of Famous Dog Breeds and Breeders' caught my eye just before I reached 636.7. No time right now for a big book like that. There were several books on dog obedience that looked quite interesting. I put the best ones in a pile and then took them to a free desk. I quickly glanced through them all and picked two that seemed to cover all of the material Leslie had talked about in the course. I returned the rest to the shelves.

No sign of Adam yet. I wondered what was taking him so long; I'd called him at least an hour ago. I went over to the Asian collection and picked out my favourite book. I was sitting in a cubicle when I heard Adam's voice as he came through the door.

"So what breed was the dog again?" asked a familiar female voice. Vanessa!

"We're not sure," Adam responded. "It was small and white. It ran away before we could get a good look."

"I know of a great book in the library that might help you find the breed... Oh, hello Autumn."

"Hello, Vanessa," I quickly replied, turning away to face Adam. "What took you so long?"

"I met up with Vanessa on the way here and you know, we were talking."

"Yes Autumn, I was hoping I could help Adam find the dog the two of you were chasing."

"Help? We really don't need help finding the dog. If we do, we'll call you." I looked down at my arms crossed across my chest. Was this defensive body language or what? I quickly put my hands down and tried to look relaxed.

Vanessa could see it was time to leave. "I'll catch you later, Adam. Bye, Autumn." She turned around, flipped her hair, smiled at Adam and quickly left the library.

"Got to talking about what, Adam? And why are you grinning like an idiot?"

"Hmmm," Adam turned to look at me. "Did you have fun at the course this morning?" he asked.

"It was really great," I replied. "Way better than I thought it was going to be. But don't think you can get off this easy, just by changing the subject on me."

"You're acting kind of funny, Autumn. Are you okay?"

I took a deep breath. "I'm fine. Let's get to work."

"So what's up? What did you want to find at the library?"

"I wanted to get some books on dog obedience and I thought we could also look for that newspaper article Mrs. Chandler mentioned. But I really thought we should check for stories and ads about missing dogs. Who knows, there might be some names of people to contact, or pictures we could use, and the two of us will work much faster than if I try to do it alone."

"Okay, where do you want to start?"

"Wendy said she'd help out when we were ready. She'll know where to look."

Adam looked at the book I was holding. "Are you reading that book again?"

'All About Shanghai - A Standard Guidebook', is the best book in the whole library.

"Do you still remember that Pidgin-English we learned?" I

asked Adam.

"You bet I do," he replied. "And I'll never forget the horrified look on Mr. Parker's face when we started to talk like that in school. He got all puffy and red and said that 'the white man used Pidgin-English as a weapon of oppression, and we should apologize to the whole class.' You told him that it was the Shanghai Chinese that invented the language and that's how they actually spoke to the English in the 1930s. I think I can still do our skit, want to give it a try?"

"Sure. You were the foreigner and I was the shopkeeper."

"My wantchee (I want)," Adam began pointing at a pretend loaf of bread. "S'pose catchee two piece can more cheap (will it be cheaper to take two)?"

I nodded my head. "One doll-o, one doll-o."

"Pay two piece (give me two). You havee walkee-walkee fish (do you have any live fish)?" Adam asked.

"So solly (sorry)," I replied. "Have got plenty something dirty rice. You wantchee (you want it)?"

"No wantchee," Adam then grabbed the two loaves of bread and said "Biembye makee pay (I'll pay later)."

"Still cracks me up," Adam laughed. "I can't believe they really talked like that."

"I know, but the guidebook says they really did."

I put the book back on the shelf and we went to get Wendy.

It took us over an hour, but we finally found the newspaper article announcing the Happy Puppy Obedience School.

"Look at this, Adam," I pointed. "It says that the school is affiliated with an American obedience school just across the border. It looks like they both started up about a month before the dogs started to go missing."

"Could be a coincidence," Adam said. "Anything else in the

article?"

"Yeah, lots. The owner's older brother owns a big diamond mine up north. He apparently provided the financing to open the school."

"I wish my brother had lots of money and was that nice to me," Adam grinned.

"Let's make a photocopy of this and then take the bus out to the beach," I said.

"Great! I think we've spent enough time indoors for one afternoon anyway. I'm all for a swim and then another snooze on the beach. It's too bad that we couldn't find any stories about the missing dogs."

We were just about to leave the library when it hit me.

"Oh no, we've been so stupid," I said thumping my forehead with the palm of my hand. "We should have been looking at the classified ads in the back of the papers as well. They always have a Missing Pets section."

"Guess we better haul out all of the old papers again," Adam sighed.

It took us another half an hour, but we ended up with the names and numbers of six different people who had taken out ads for missing dogs.

"Still no white dog," I said.

"It figures. Anyway, at least we have a place to start. Maybe one of the people on this list will have heard about the dog."

"Would you mind calling them?" Adam was very good at talking to total strangers on the phone and getting important information from them, which is why I always recruited him into doing it.

Adam smiled. "I'll start calling when we get back from the beach and let you know tomorrow afternoon if I find anything."

秋玉

9

Shanghai, 1934. We are floating in a dream above the great, sprawling city. As we look down, three very special young girls suddenly come into focus.

Amy. She stands at the entrance to the British Consulate, flaming red hair blowing in the wind.

"Promise to be careful, Amy," cautions a distinguished looking, silver-haired gentleman.

"Oh Father, I can look out for myself."

"And you've amply proven it over the years. However with the Japanese invading Shanghai, you need to be extra vigilant. Try not to attract too much attention."

She hugs her father and ties a dull gray kerchief over her red hair. She hops on her bicycle and speeds south along the Bund, the main street of Shanghai's International Settlement. She passes the Public Gardens where the sign at the gate says 'No Dogs, No Chinese Allowed.' No matter how many times Amy has seen this sign it always makes her mad. She darts at the big red-turbaned Sikh guard, pretending to knock him down. After narrowly missing a slow moving oxcart and several coolies carrying their loads, she's finally on her way to the North Gate of Nantao, Shanghai's old China City.

Soo-Lin. The Creek-Child has lived on a boat in Soochow Creek her entire life. Her younger brother is usually tied to her waist to prevent him from falling into the foul liquid that runs through the creek.

"I have errands to run, Honorable Uncle. Can I tie Didi up over here? He promises to be quiet as you do your t'ai chi."

Soo-Lin's uncle answers without pausing as he performs a tricky hand movement followed by a graceful kick to an imaginary target. "Certainly, Soo-Lin. Make sure you return before dark, though."

Soo-Lin lightly boat-hops across to the shoreline and then blends into the crowd walking down Thibet Road towards the Shanghai Race Club. At Avenue Edward VII she turns east and also heads to the North Gate of Nantao.

Qiu Yu. Long raven black hair and a four-dimple smile. She traveled the world with her parents before a tragic incident took their lives. Auntie Shu-Shu feels she does her best to bring up what to her is a very difficult and precocious child.

"I'm going out for a while, Auntie."

"If you're not back by six o'clock, the stray dogs will have your dinner."

"Oh Auntie, how would I know now what time I'll return? Who can say where the day will lead?"

"Qiu Yu, you listen to your old Auntie. I will not help you if you get into trouble of any kind. Do you hear me?"

"Yes, Auntie, good-bye!"

Auntie Shu-Shu's house is in a newer neighbourhood just outside the walls of the old China City. At one time it was Qiu Yu's parents' home, but no longer. Qiu walks along the road that follows the crumbling wall until she reaches the North Gate.

The three girls are about to meet at their secret garden.

After arriving at the North Gate, they each head south, keeping to the main streets. The alleyways are lined with low houses. Long poles, bending under the weight of washing spread out to dry, jut out from under the eaves of the dwellings. Upright, gilded signboards hang over the open-fronted shops.

There are craftspeople everywhere, selling clothing of all kinds. Everything is made of silk in bright colours. There are dresses, jackets and even shoes in all shades of red, yellow, green and blue. The air in the open market is filled with the smells of fish, drying seaweed, herbs, and vegetables frying in hot oil. Through it all drifts the smell of human filth and over-flowing sewers that follows you wherever you are in the city.

At the back of the Confucius Temple they turn right down a small alley. Nineteen steps and there on the right, near the ground, is a small hole in the back wall. One by one they squeeze through the hole to enter into the back of the garden. Stalks of bamboo, thick as a man's thigh and over thirty feet high, hide the hole on the other side of the wall. An overgrown trail leads out from the grove to three stepping stones that cross a narrow stream. A marble bridge carved with intricate designs connects to an island with a miniature, moss-roofed pagoda – here at last, is their special meeting place.

Qiu helped Amy through the hole in the temple wall. "How come you're so late?"

"There were roadblocks everywhere. I had to take all sorts of detours until I reached the North Gate."

Soo-Lin gave Amy a worried look. "What's happening, Amy?"

"Yes, what's the latest news?" Qiu chimed in.

"Japanese planes flew over the city and bombed the main railway station. My dad says that entire neighbourhoods are raging with fire and there is no hope of controlling it. Japanese marines have landed in Chapei district and thousands of people are evacuating into the International Settlement. We watched from the top of the consulate and saw the evacuees flooding in. The flames rose hundreds of feet into the air. People had snatched whatever household belongings they could carry and they were running for their lives. It was really frightening. My dad says that the Chinese are talking about resisting, but some of the English officers don't really believe they can."

"I saw Chinese soldiers that looked as though they were fifteen-year-old boys," added Soo-Lin. "The ones at the back of the line only had tennis shoes and they were so scared they were holding hands like schoolboys do."

Amy looked at the other girls. "If only there was some way we could help out!"

秋玉

10

It was nine forty-five exactly, and we were back at Happy Puppy for our second class.

"Thanks, Mom."

"Have fun!"

Last night I'd taken a look through the dog obedience books from the library. I'd picked up a couple of tips that Watson and I had practiced. We could turn as a team and I'd already taught him how to shake a paw. It was actually easy once you knew what to do.

I had gotten Watson to sit and then I started to pet him gently on the side of his chin. It took lots of patience, because I had to wait until he lifted his paw, even slightly. The dog has to make the first move, so it can take a while. When he finally lifted his foot, I took the paw and shook it, praising him vigorously. It took about twenty or thirty times but then he knew the trick. The other important thing was to tell him 'shake,' or 'shake hands,' every time he did it.

In fact, it worked almost too well for Watson. All morning he wouldn't stop lifting his paw for me!

Ms. Greasy Hair was still sitting at the front desk. She didn't bother to look up as we walked by. I bet she hadn't moved an inch since yesterday morning.

We turned into the meeting room. "Hi, Leslie! Guess what Watson can do now?"

Leslie smiled. "Show me."

"Watson, sit. Good boy, Watson, shake a paw."

On cue he raised his left front leg so Leslie could shake it.

"Glad to meet you, fine sir," Leslie said as she shook his paw. "Well done, you two! Someone must have been practicing last night."

I winked at her. "Just a bit. He really is a good dog, when he's not being lazy."

"Most dogs aren't lazy by nature, they're just bored. Herding dogs like Watson and Sadie are bred to work all day. You have to keep them busy."

"It was hard to find the time when I was at school."

"Then use your summer vacation to make sure he gets lots of exercise. Develop a routine you can use when you're back at school, especially for the weekends."

"I'd love to take him hiking, but he's always wandering off on me. He doesn't listen when I try to call him back."

"Like I said yesterday, by the end of the week I bet you won't have that problem any more."

Leslie stood up to greet the other students as they arrived. Once everyone had shown up, we headed outside to the training area.

I was really glad we had practiced last night. And I wished I had brought my dad's camcorder to class because it would have made a great submission to Funny Home Videos. I've never seen such a bunch of uncoordinated people. We'd be walking in a big circle and Leslie would call out 'turn.' We were supposed to gracefully turn with our dogs and head back in the opposite direction. The first few times, people and dogs were crashing into each other as they tried to turn. One older woman with a Golden Retriever actually tripped over her dog and fell flat on her butt. She turned, her dog didn't and down she went. Her dog ran back to see if she was okay, a big worried expression on his face.

At the first break, I let Watson get a big drink of water and then we went over to sit down by one of the blue plastic tunnels. I could see the front entrance of the kennel from where I was sitting. The door opened and a big man poked his head out. A black lab with white feet tried to sneak out between his legs but he quickly grabbed it by the collar and pushed it back inside. He looked over with a big grin on his face and then he waved at us.

When the class was almost finished, Leslie called us all over for another little demonstration.

"A dog has a big part of its brain devoted to smelling. Some scientists believe that dogs can remember a smell just like you and I remember a picture." I smiled. That was exactly what Mrs. Chandler had said the other night.

"I've hidden an old teddy bear of Sadie's somewhere in the training area," she continued. "Watch this. Sadie, go find your bear!"

Sadie took off like a shot. She sniffed around the tunnel, then the ramp that was another five feet away. She came back half way between the two and started to dig. Up came the bear and Sadie proudly raced back to her owner.

"Good girl, Sadie, well done."

"Nearly any dog can do that trick," she said. "I've got a handout on scent tracking if anyone is interested. It might be something to practice if you're not busy tonight! See you all tomorrow. Have a great day."

I grabbed a copy of the handout and then we went out to get our ride home.

Adam came over after lunch.

"Have a good time?" he asked.

"We learned some great stuff today. And get this, I think I saw one of the missing dogs that Mrs. Chandler described."

"No way, where?"

"I didn't think about it at the time, but there's a kennel behind the school and I just got a peek at a black lab with white feet before this big guy pushed it back inside."

"Are you sure it was the same dog?"

"It sure looked right, but the fellow at the kennel seemed pretty friendly, so I just don't know. Any luck with your calls last night?"

"Not really. Five of the people had found their dogs already. The sixth one gave me a description of her dog, which I've written down. She also suggested we call the S.P.C.A. and see if they have any more information on the missing dogs."

"We should do that right now," I said.

I grabbed the phone book and looked up the number for the local S.P.C.A. Adam made the call.

"Hello, my name is Adam and I saw a stray dog running through the park the other day. Do you have any pictures of dogs that have gone missing lately? You do? Great, could we come down and take a look?"

Adam said thanks and put down the phone. "We're in luck, Autumn. They have a big notice board for people to put up posters of their missing pets. She said we could come down any time and have a look at it. There are all kinds of missing dogs on it right now!"

I let Mom know where we were going and then we grabbed our

bikes and pedaled down the hill as fast as we could go.

"Did you bring any change?" I shouted at Adam. "We might want to do some photocopying."

"She said they already had copies of the posters. People usually drop off stacks of them."

We locked our bikes and went inside. There was almost a whole wall covered with missing animal posters. On a rickety table beside the notice board were the extra copies.

"I don't believe it," said a very disappointed Adam. "I don't see one picture that looks like our little white dog. There must be over twenty other dogs here, though."

"Why don't we take one copy of each poster and keep them with us?" I suggested. "That way if we see another stray dog we can look at the posters for a match."

We picked up the copies and neatly placed them in Adam's backpack.

"Tomorrow I'll ask our instructor Leslie about Happy Puppy's kennel, just in case I was right about the dog I saw."

"And I'll call the people on these posters," Adam said. "Maybe one of them can help us. Someone must be missing that little white dog and I'm going to find them."

We both got on our bikes at the same time. "Race you home!" I said and charged up the hill as fast as I could pedal.

秋玉

11

The Bund was the heart of Shanghai, perhaps the single most famous street in all of China. It curved along the riverbank for nearly a mile from the Shanghai Club at the corner of the Avenue Edward VII to the British Consulate just before the Garden Bridge. Qiu Yu, special agent on assignment in Shanghai, kept to the shadows as she tailed the courier.

Okay, she wasn't really a secret agent, but Soo-Lin and Qiu were following somebody who looked pretty suspicious. Amy, Soo-Lin and Qiu had been eating a snack of warm dumplings by the Garden Bridge when they saw an American cross over from what used to be the U.S. side of the Soochow Creek.

Soo-Lin noticed him first and remarked, "I thought all of the Americans had moved out to avoid a confrontation with the Japanese?"

The American had quickly passed a brown paper package to the tall Chinese boy Soo-Lin and Qiu were now following. Amy had gone up to the roof of the British Consulate to try and see where the American was going. Everyone had agreed to meet back at the Garden Bridge in an hour.

"Boy, it's hot," Qiu swore under her breath. The summer air made her feel like she was walking around inside a great big oven. Qiu signaled to Soo-Lin to take over while she gulped some water from her canteen.

It was easy to stay out of sight, but it was taking both girls to keep up with the quarry. Most of the trading houses had their own godowns, or warehouses, towering over the pavement. The street was filled wall-to-wall with pedestrians, messengers, businessmen, and hawkers, all casting around for something to either buy or sell. The hawkers would beseech passers-by with guttural cries to accept a cold drink, examine a pair of Chinese slippers, or try their fountain pens. The buzzing knots of people made the heat seem even worse.

Dozens of tiny stalls held mysterious cooking implements. There was the smell of noodles cooking, and the sharper whiff of Szechwan food laced with chilies. Soo-Lin had once boasted that she could smell her way across China just by walking down the Bund.

There were beggars everywhere, often pitifully deformed. Legless people sat on small home-made platforms with tiny wheels, the blind were led by small boys. Among them were survivors of the Russian Communist Revolution, known as White Russians. Dignified even in poverty, many waited patiently by the side of the road, hat in hand, looking for a few coins to keep them going.

Soo-Lin and Qiu had to walk carefully to avoid the coolies carrying huge bales hanging like scales on bamboo poles. The poles were arched across aching backs, each man with his eyes fixed on the ground ahead where his next footstep would fall, and giving short, sharp cries of warning as he tried to pass without altering his gait.

Qiu caught up to Soo-Lin, who had suddenly stopped and was peering out from behind a silk hawker's stall.

"Can you still see him?" Qiu whispered.

"He went inside the Bank of China. I think he's just standing beside the front door. He looked around like he thought he was being followed and then ducked into the bank."

"There's no way he could have seen us," Qiu said. "No one would notice two kids in this crowd."

"Maybe he thought someone else was following him," Soo-Lin suggested.

"Oh, oh, there he goes," Qiu softly exclaimed. "You take the waterfront and I'll keep to this side of the street. We'll meet again in front of the North China Daily News."

Concentrating on catching up, Qiu almost tripped on a boot-black boy pointing scornfully at someone's already highly polished shoes. She then had to dodge a bearded professional letter-writer with his minuscule desk and pots of ink. Qiu decided to follow along behind a silk hawker carrying three rolls of silk in deep bags slung round his neck. He made for good cover.

Soo-Lin was walking on the far side of a dust-covered water buffalo pulling an ancient cart with great wooden wheels. The tall Chinese boy stopped in front of the Cathay Hotel and pretended to tie his shoes. The Cathay was a magnificent ten-storey concrete building on almost an acre of land. Amy had been inside once and said the rooms all had marble baths with silver taps. She had eaten a fancy dinner in one of the modern restaurants before attending a tea dance in the famous ballroom.

Qiu stopped to look at some silk scarves until the boy moved on again. When they reached the North China Daily News, he was nowhere in sight.

"Did you see him go inside?" Qiu asked.

"I'm not sure," Soo-Lin replied. "Want me to peek through the front window and see if he's there?"

"Good idea, I'll keep a lookout from here."

Soo-Lin was back in less than a minute.

"He's there all right, but he's in handcuffs and two Japanese soldiers are questioning him."

"I guess that's the end of it. We better go see if Amy has any news."

Amy could barely contain herself when the girls arrived.

"Where have you been? I was about to ask my dad to go get some help. The Japanese are taking over all of Hongkew district," she began. "The American we saw is on our side. He's been spying on the Japanese and sending maps of their troop locations out to the Chinese army."

Qiu quickly filled Amy in on their pursuit of the courier, ending with his capture.

"I guess we weren't the only ones to see the exchange on the bridge."

"There must be a better way to get the information out," Qiu said.

"I'm sure there is," Amy replied, "but no one at the consulate has thought of it yet. My father says they've been racking their brains to come up with a better courier system. It has a top priority."

Qiu was staring out at the boats in Soochow Creek. Soo-Lin lived on one of those boats, although she would never point it out to them. Whole families had been conceived, born, lived and died on the small boats without ever walking on land. She could see a dog playing with a young boy on one of the boats. The dog was giving her an idea.

"Don't laugh," Qiu said. "But I've just got this crazy idea. Amy, you said that you wished we could somehow help out, right? I mean, help by getting information to the Chinese Army?"

"Sure!" The girls waited to hear.

"Well, here it is, but don't say anything until I'm done. We get Soo-Lin to borrow a dog from one of the families on the boats. We train the dog as a courier and have it carry messages and stuff around the city. Dogs are smart enough to do all sorts of amazing things. No one would look twice at a stray dog wandering down the street."

"That's crazy!" Amy said. "It will never work. None of us has ever had a dog before."

"Never mind that. How about it, Soo-Lin? Do you think someone would lend us their dog?"

"No problem, especially if we never bring it back. 'If there are too many dogs, not enough food for people' as my Uncle would say."

"That settles it, then. All we have to do now is figure out how to train the dog and we're all set."

"All?" Amy exclaimed. "Come on, Qiu Yu, none of us knows anything about training a dog."

"We'll just have to find someone who can teach us, then. Agreed?"

"Okay with me," Soo-Lin said.

"I guess so. We have to try something to help out," Amy conceded.

秋玉

12

It was only Wednesday morning, but Watson and I were already getting the hang of this obedience business. In fact, Watson appeared to be really enjoying the training and we were already looking like the stars of the class.

Before we started, Leslie had us all gather around.

"We're going to begin by reviewing everything we have covered so far," she said. "That should take us up to the first break. After that, we're going to work on two new commands, 'down' and 'down-stay.' Everybody ready? Okay, let's go!"

At the first break, I went over to ask Leslie the question about the Happy Puppy Kennel that Adam and I had come up with last night. Adam was going to call and pretend he wanted to board his dog at the kennel. I was going to ask Leslie the same question and then we'd compare our answers afterwards.

"My mom wanted me to ask you about kenneling a friend's dog while they're on vacation," I said. "Do you know how much it costs? Do they need to book very far in advance?"

"I asked the owner when I started working here, and he said that it was $50 a day and they needed a week's notice. There always seem to be lots of dogs there, although I haven't had a look inside lately. I've been so busy teaching classes I haven't had time."

"Okay, thanks, I'll let my mom know." I hated to lie since she'd been so nice to me, but Adam and I had agreed it was best not to give away too much to anyone even remotely affiliated with the Happy Puppy Kennel.

Between the first and second breaks, the fellow I'd seen yesterday at the kennel came by to watch our class. He seemed to be watching Watson and the German Shepherd cross with special interest.

Leslie was showing us how to do a proper 'down' with her dog Sadie.

"There are many occasions when the down command will help your dog enjoy the activities around him without getting into trouble," she began. "Just remember that 'down' and 'stay' are not corrections. You should still use 'no' for that."

"Is there a hand signal that goes with it?" I asked.

"Bring your left hand up above the dog's eye level and slightly to the right of his head. Keep it flattened, fingers together, palm down. Give the dog the verbal command 'down' as you begin to lower your hand towards the ground. As your hand goes down, it will press on the leash and help push him down."

At our second break, the guy from the kennel wandered over to talk to the German Shepherd's owner. He was petting the dog and being very chummy.

I caught Leslie's attention.

"Who's the big guy?"

"His name is Eddie, he runs the kennel. I think he used to train terriers a few years back. Eddie usually checks out how the training is going on the third or fourth day. Looks like he wants to meet Watson next."

"Good morning, Leslie. Can you introduce me to your young friend?"

"Eddie, this is Autumn and her dog Watson."

"Hello, Autumn. I've been watching you and your dog. He sure is a smart fellow. I consider myself a good judge of dogs and I think yours has real talent."

"Thank you," I said.

"Would you mind if I tried putting Watson through the obstacle course?" Eddie asked.

"I don't know," I hesitated. "Watson's never done anything like that before."

"He'll be fine," Leslie said.

"And I have lots of experience doing this too," Eddie said. "I promise I'll take it real easy with him."

"Well, I guess it'll be okay if Leslie says so. Watson, follow Eddie and do what he says."

Eddie took Watson over to the start of the course. He had Watson sit on his left side. He waited several seconds and then shouted, "Go!" They both took off running full out.

Straight off there were two jumps to go over. Eddie said 'over' and 'over' as he made an upward motion with his left hand. Watson cleared the metre high jumps with room to spare. Next up was a big two metre high 'A' frame ramp. Up the ramp, 'wait' at the top and then 'slow' coming down the other side.

My heart was in my throat as I watched.

Another jump and then a long, narrow ramp over a pool of water. Wow. Down the ramp, around and through a tunnel, two more jumps and they were done.

"You're a very lucky girl," Eddie said when he got back. "He's a smart dog and learns quickly. Not many dogs do that well the first time. Thanks for letting me try him out."

"I can't believe Watson just did that," was all I could blurt out.

"You might want to think about taking our advanced course later this summer," Eddie suggested. "I think Watson is more than ready and he is definitely willing."

"Thank you, I'll talk to my mom about the course when she picks me up."

"I hope to see both of you later this summer. It's one of the few classes I still get to teach around here. Good-bye Autumn, and good boy Watson, I hope to see you again." And with that Eddie left the training area.

The end of the class arrived before we knew it.

"Just two more classes to go," Leslie announced. "Tomorrow we will learn 'come' and 'fetch' and on Friday we'll have some fun on the obstacle course and then do a final test for your diplomas. Remember, everyone should practice what we've covered so far for at least fifteen minutes!"

Poor Watson looked absolutely pooped as he dragged himself into the back seat of Mom's car.

"What happened to Watson?" Mom asked.

"Eddie who runs the kennel took Watson through the obstacle course. You wouldn't believe how well Watson did, I'm so proud of him. Eddie said he thought Watson would be ready for the advanced training course. What do you think Mom?"

"We'll see. I thought there were other things you had planned for the summer. Does this mean you are enjoying the course?"

"Yeah, it's been great so far."

Adam came over right after lunch. He was bursting to tell me what he had found out.

"You'll never guess in a million years what happened," he said as he came through the back door.

"I give. Tell me before you explode."

"I called the school and this woman answers the phone. She almost sounded like she was asleep and maybe I'd woken her up."

"You probably did," I interrupted, thinking of Ms. Greasy Hair.

"I told her I was phoning from out of town and that I needed to board my dog while I stayed with my Uncle for a few days. Get this. She told me they don't use the kennel anymore, because it was losing too much money. She said the kennel is closed and there are no dogs inside. She gave me a couple of other places to try calling instead."

"No way. Leslie just told me the kennel is still in business. That's what she's been told by the owner, anyway, and I've seen the dogs myself. This is getting very odd, Adam. How did your other phone calls go?"

"Pretty slow until I got to the 12th poster in my pile. It was a Mrs. Norman just over on 3rd Street and she had recently lost her one-year-old Golden Retriever. She made a comment that really got me thinking. She said 'I was especially upset that Maggie disappeared since we had just finished a training course at the Happy Puppy Obedience School.'"

"Wow!"

"I then called back all the people I had already talked to. You won't believe it, but five of them had taken the same course you're taking. Within two weeks of graduating, their dogs went missing. Another two people had put their dogs into the kennel and they also went missing several weeks afterwards. So, what do you think we should do now?"

"I think we better take a closer look at Happy Puppy's kennel operation," I replied. "How about tonight?"

"I can't do it tonight," Adam said. "We have company coming

over in about an hour. Tomorrow?"

"No, we're going downtown to see a new play. Once my class is over, Mom wants to make an afternoon of it. Guess it'll have to wait until Friday."

"It looks like we don't have much choice," Adam admitted.

"Yeah. In the meantime, I'll keep a sharp eye out for anything suspicious during the final two classes," I said.

"And I'll try to reach the rest of the people on my list. Maybe something else will turn up."

As I lay in bed Wednesday night my mind was swirling. The Happy Puppy Obedience School appeared to have some odd things going on, but our instructor Leslie and Eddie at the kennel didn't seem like the kind of people to be mixed up in any sort of trouble. Leslie had been so helpful. She had given me extra exercises to do for 'fetch' and 'go find', and she had used Watson for demonstrations when Sadie wasn't close by.

I thought I had seen a dog at the kennel that looked like one of the missing ones, but now I wasn't so sure. Why steal the dogs in the first place? Who was the owner of the little white dog? What was in the backpack he was carrying?

These were the many unanswered questions in my mind as I drifted off to sleep...

秋玉

13

Amy had mentioned Qiu's courier idea to her father. He thought it was a super idea and said he would check around for someone who knew how to train dogs. He soon found a White Russian named Sergei Ivanovitch who offered to help. Sergei had trained police dogs before fleeing a Russian firing squad during the Bolshevik Revolution. One of the fires set by the Japanese planes had damaged Sergei's restaurant and with the current situation in the city, it could be weeks before it was repaired. Fortunately for the girls, this meant he now had some free time to spare. Sergei offered to help train the dog until his restaurant was rebuilt. Now all they needed was the right dog.

"We need very special doggie," he said. "Not just any one will do."

"What do you mean?" Amy asked, trying not to giggle at his accent. "Shouldn't most dogs be able to carry our messages across the city?"

"Nyet, doggies will only remember the image for about 20 seconds, this makes it difficult to tell them where to go. It is better to have him follow scent trail. The dog we choose might have to follow trail over long distance. If we're lucky with weather, and get dew or fog, trail will be easy to follow. If we have typical heat and wind, odours are quickly removed and will be hard for doggie to follow."

"We have a bunch of dogs to choose from," Soo-Lin said. "How can we test them to find the best one?"

"I, Sergei, will devise simple test to help us pick best one. Come children, let us go."

Soo-Lin took the four of them down beside the boats in Soochow Creek. She got some of the nearby children to help round up all of the likely candidates.

Sergei held his nose with two fingers. "This creek, it smells very strong today. We will have to test doggies in nearby Public Gardens."

"But Soo-Lin and I can't go into the Gardens," Qiu protested.

Sergei looked at the girls. "I have idea. You and Soo-Lin bring each of the doggies in turn from creek to park. Amy and I will do testing. Okay?"

Sergei put some of the putrid smelling muck from the edge of Soochow Creek into a bucket. He then dipped empty bullet casings into the muck so they would be covered with the scent. He laid a trail through the park by placing the bullets on the ground at a certain distance. Amy was waiting at the end of the scent trail with a treat for the dog that was successful.

After bringing all sorts of dogs back and forth from the creek, Sergei and Amy came out with a skinny little white dog that had bright green eyes.

"Where did that dog come from?" Soo-Lin asked. "He wasn't one of the dogs we brought over."

"You'll never believe it," Amy exclaimed. "This little dog showed up out of nowhere. Sergei watched him follow the scent trail to the exact spot where I was hiding."

"Yes," Sergei said. "This is very smart doggie. He will do."

"What should we call him?" Amy asked.

"How about naming him Lucky?" Qiu suggested.

"You will need luck, this is good name," Sergei agreed.

Sergei proceeded to teach the three girls the basics of training Lucky to follow a scent trail. He wrapped up his short lecture with some final thoughts.

"Most important is to identify wind direction and speed to better understand and anticipate doggie's response to the scent trail. Ask the doggie to search between two given points, identify trail and then proceed in the proper direction.

"When time comes to do for real, design your tracks to strengthen weak points and downwind turns. If possible, have communication with doggie to assist in following the track.

"I had once a very special doggie that tracked an escaped prisoner in torrential rain, through water up to six inches deep, over two and half hours after the track was laid. I think that what you want doggie for is much easier than tracking. Please come see me if you have more questions. Dosvodonya, excuse me, I mean to say good-bye, my young friends."

The girls took Lucky back to their secret garden to do the training. They ignored occasional strange looks as they walked Lucky through the Chinese City using an old piece of rope as a leash.

As Sergei had instructed them, they started with a collection of scented and unscented articles. To scent the articles, they rubbed their hands on the items so they had a body 'scent' on them. The unscented articles had to be handled very carefully, so they didn't put any scent on them.

"I've got a scarf and a pocketbook," Amy said.

"Here's some women's gloves and an old bottle I found," Soo-Lin added.

"And I have this handkerchief and a set of keys," Qiu said.

The idea was to put out a pair of scented and unscented items and make sure Lucky went to the scented one each time. The girls drew straws and Amy came up the winner, so she got to give Lucky the commands.

"Go find," she'd say, and each time he correctly went to the scented item.

"Boy, he's sure smart," Amy said admiringly.

"Let's try something harder," Qiu suggested. "Soo-Lin and I will each take one of the scented items and go hide in the garden. Amy, you count to fifty and then tell Lucky which item to go find."

Qiu took the gloves, ran out from the pagoda and found a great hiding spot behind a sea of blooming lotus flowers, chrysanthemums, and orchids. Soo-Lin took the gloves and disappeared behind one of the two moon gates in the garden.

Qiu heard Amy tell Lucky to 'go find the gloves.' He came out like a streak of lightning, went straight into the pond and tried to catch the white and gold carp that were lazily swimming about.

"Oh no, Lucky! Get out of the pond," Amy yelled. "Bad, bad dog."

"Guess that was a failure," Qiu said, running over to Amy.

Soo-Lin was quiet for several minutes. "Lucky seems to like fish. Why don't we use some fish guts as the scent? I can bring some next time."

It took several days of practicing and trying out different ideas, but they finally got Lucky to follow a scent trail through the garden and find them no matter how well hidden they were. In the end they decided to use Sergei's old bullet casings covered in fish guts. Sergei figured they could plant them along the Bund – no one would notice them or wonder what was going on.

Sergei also gave the girls a dog whistle to use.

"People can't hear whistle, but little doggies can. Use whistle if Lucky loses scent and you need to get him back on track."

Soo-Lin and Qiu placed the scented bullets along the Bund, starting at the Garden Bridge, all the way around to the wharves opposite the Customs House.

Facing the Customs House was a monument to Sir Robert Hart, an early Inspector General of the Chinese Maritime Customs in Shanghai and the one-time guardian of the heir apparent to the throne of China. Qiu hid behind the statue and Soo-Lin went back about halfway with the whistle. At precisely two o'clock, Amy released Lucky and told him to go find Qiu. He had a small package attached to his collar and Qiu had a nice, fat treat waiting for him.

Barely ten minutes later, a panting Lucky came running up to the monument.

"Woof," he said.

"Oh Lucky!" Qiu cried out. "What a good boy you are." She gave him the treat and affectionately rubbed his ears. "I'm so proud of you."

Amy and Soo-Lin arrived out of breath, but happy.

"He was amazing," they both agreed.

"And I didn't even have to use the whistle!" added Soo-Lin.

They were ready to try it for real next time!

"Amy," Qiu said with a big grin, "I think you can tell your dad that we're all set to give Lucky a try with the secret messages."

秋玉

14

After our breakfast Friday morning, I gave Watson a special brushing for our final class. I couldn't believe the improvement in Watson with just four classes. I knew it had a lot to do with my confidence, because I knew what to tell Watson and how to say it. He seemed to like me being alpha dog. Anyway, Mom and Dad were really happy that he was listening so well. I gave Watson a great, big hug for being such a good dog.

"Is it all right if I watch today?" Mom asked.

"Sure! Leslie did say that it would be okay to have a guest for today's class."

"And you decided not to tell me?" Mom raised her eyebrows.

"I didn't think you would want to come."

"Autumn, I'm very proud of what you've accomplished with Watson. Of course I'd like to watch your class today. I'd also like to bring the camcorder so Dad can see your performance."

I gave Mom a hug. "I would love to have you come and watch the class."

"Thank you, Autumn. Now we'd better get going, we don't want to be late."

"Right Mom. Better to be early," I muttered to myself.

At the school, Mom parked the car and Watson and I walked ahead.

I did a double take as we walked by the front office. Instead of Ms. Greasy Hair, there was a very plump, older man in the front office. He sat with his feet up on the desk, reading a newspaper.

Who could he be? With Mom coming up behind me, I didn't have time to stop and find out more. I'd have to check on the way out.

"Morning," he called out cheerfully.

"Morning," Mom replied.

"What a friendly person," Mom said as she caught up. "Are they all so nice here?"

What could I say? That this wasn't the regular receptionist and she was a bag? "Seems that way."

I received an even bigger shock as we walked out into the training area. There was Vanessa, talking and laughing with Leslie.

"Hi, Autumn," Vanessa called out.

I feebly waved back.

"Looks like your friend wants to talk to you," observed Mom. "I'll go stand with the other guests."

That didn't leave me much choice. I put on my happy smile. "Good morning, Vanessa. What are you doing here?"

"I kept telling you that I knew something about dogs. I was one of Leslie's first students just after the obedience school opened."

"Blondie received first prize, as I recall," added Leslie.

"She sure did. I was just asking Leslie if she might have seen her. Blondie went missing yesterday and my whole family is worried sick."

"I'm pretty confident she will show up soon," said Leslie, "I wouldn't worry too much about it."

"Thanks, Leslie. I'll let you know if we find her. Autumn, can we talk privately for a minute?"

"Don't see why not. Have I got time before the class starts, Leslie?"

"Sure. Catch you later, Vanessa!"

We walked over to one of the fruit trees in complete silence. Watson lay down in the shade and watched us from between his front paws.

"Okay, Vanessa, what did you want to talk about?"

Vanessa seemed at a loss for words. Finally she said, "Adam's great, isn't he?"

Well, I had to agree with that. "Yes, he is," I said.

"Is he your boyfriend?" Vanessa asked.

I laughed. "Of course not. Adam is just a really good friend."

"I wasn't sure, Autumn. You two seem so close all the time." Vanessa was smiling now.

There wasn't anything going on with me and Adam was there? Or was there? That would sure explain why I was getting so upset when Adam paid any attention to Vanessa. Why hadn't I seen it coming? Was I that stupid? And now Vanessa was all happy that Adam wasn't my boyfriend. I needed some time to think this over.

"Whoops, Leslie is calling us. I'm going to have to go. I hope you find your dog soon, Vanessa."

"Thanks! I'm sure he'll turn up by tomorrow."

Watson and I hurried back to join the others. Quite a crowd had shown up for the final class. Leslie had all the visitors stand off to the side while she showed us the basics of the obstacle course. Once again, Watson was amazing as he flew through the course. It happened so fast that I was glad Mom was there to capture it all on tape.

Some of the other owners didn't have it so easy.

The Bearded Collie that had been doing so well all week got stuck at the top of the 'A' frame ramp. She was so afraid of coming back down that eventually her owner had to climb the ramp and push her down the other side.

After everyone had more or less successfully traversed the course, Leslie called us over to explain the test we would be taking.

"For those of you who go on to show your dogs, this test is just the first of many steps. For the rest of you, I hope passing the test will give you a feeling of satisfaction for what you've accomplished this week. I've asked Eddie, whom some of you have already met, and Mr. Frank Dixon, the owner's brother, to be the judges this morning."

No way! The plump guy I'd seen in the front office was the one who had financed the school. The diamond business must be pretty slow if he had time to hang around and judge our performance.

"Each of you will have to come up to this line," Leslie continued. "Tell your dog to 'sit.' Then say 'stand', 'wait' for five seconds then 'heel', and walk to the red cone that's about thirty feet away. 'Turn' at the cone and come back half-way. Have your dog 'down-stay' and walk back to the line. Count to thirty and then say 'come.' When your dog reaches you, have them 'sit' on your left side, both of you facing the course."

With a few minor mistakes, everyone passed the test. Best of all, Watson received the first place ribbon for having the highest score.

"Look at what we won," I beamed, showing off the blue ribbon to Mom.

"You two were a great team out there. I felt like crying, it was so beautiful to see," Mom said, still choking back the tears.

I went over to thank Leslie for teaching the course.

"I really appreciate that, Autumn. I hope I'll be seeing you again." She knelt down to rub Watson under the chin. "Watson is ready for the advanced training course. You should seriously think about taking it this summer."

"I will! This was a great course for both of us and I want to learn more."

When we got home, I called Adam and told him to come over right away.

"Look," I said holding up the ribbon. "We got first prize! And Mom has it all on videotape."

"Hey, congratulations! Can we watch the tape?" Adam stopped and looked at my face. "But you didn't have me come over just for that, did you? What else happened?"

"Mr. Dixon, the owner's brother, was there today. And Vanessa was there, too. Her dog went missing and she was asking Leslie if she might have seen her. You know, other than Ms. Greasy Hair, everyone has been so friendly and nice all week. It's hard to believe that anything bad is going on there."

"Is Vanessa okay? Maybe I should call her."

"Great," I mumbled under my breath. "Let's concentrate on finding the white dog first," I said out loud. "I still think there's something funny going on at Happy Puppy. We have nothing to lose by watching the obedience school tonight."

"I suppose you're right. I'll give Vanessa a call later."

"Do you still have all those posters with you?" I asked, through gritted teeth. "If our hunch about the kennel is right, we'll need the posters to identify the missing dogs."

"Got them right here in my pack," he replied, patting the backpack. "What time do you want to meet?"

"How about seven? It will still be light enough to see. We can borrow my dad's binoculars and watch from the high point of Diefenbaker Park. It has a great view. You can see all the way out to the bay and we'll never be spotted from up there."

"I sure hope we see something," Adam said. "I have this funny feeling that we're right, but we don't have much to go on."

"I know, I was thinking the same thing as I fell asleep the other night. All we have are a handful of slim clues that all seem to point to the Happy Puppy Obedience School."

"And we still don't know who owns the little white dog. It's been a week and we've found nothing."

"You've just reminded me of something. Want to hear it?"

"Sure."

I told him about training a dog to carry secret messages around Shanghai. I figured it would be pretty easy to lay a scent trail for a dog to follow and tell them to 'go find.'

"Your stories about Shanghai are something else, Autumn!" Adam was usually a supportive audience, but today he was focused on our real mystery. "We need to see where the dogs go when they're wearing the backpacks," he continued. "Do you have any ideas about what they might be carrying?"

"No, but how about this? I bet we can teach Watson to follow a scent trail. Maybe we can even get him to find the white dog."

"Could we?" asked Adam.

"Won't know until we try," I replied. "Watson! Watson, come."

What a difference a week makes. He'd been sleeping on his back under our apple tree. When I said 'come', he jumped up and came running over.

"Good boy, Watson, good come."

I went into the house and grabbed an old stuffed teddy bear that Watson loved to play with.

"Adam, you keep Watson distracted while I go and hide the bear."

I started with an easy one. I put the bear behind a planter at the edge of the patio. I took a different route back to try and throw Watson off.

"Okay, Watson, go find your bear," I said.

He sniffed the air, hesitated for a second and then dashed over to the planter.

Adam looked totally amazed. "That's incredible," was all he could say.

We tried a couple of harder hiding places in the yard and each time he found the bear without any problems.

"Let's take him to the park and try it," Adam suggested. "Maybe he'll even pick up the white dog's trail."

"I don't think so, the smells will be long gone by now. Plus there's no way to tell Watson what to look for."

We hid Watson's bear all over the park and it wasn't until the wind picked up that he finally wasn't able to find it.

"Wow," said Adam. "I can see that if you have the right dog, it wouldn't take too much training to turn him into a search and rescue dog."

"I think finding a toy teddy bear and following a trail are very different," I said. "But I'm sure we could get Watson to follow a scent trail with a bit more work."

"Whoops, it's almost dinner time. We'd better hurry home."

"And we still have to get ready for tonight. Let's go, Watson," I called out.

秋玉

15

I'd been so busy all week that I hadn't found any free time to check my email. I was hoping I'd received a reply from the jewelers in Shanghai. I had sent them the message with the picture of my jade pendant almost a week ago. I hoped that the twenty minutes left until Adam and I were going to meet would be enough time to check my email.

"Oh no," I gasped. I had a hundred and fifty-five email messages, most of them from the Sisters of China mailing list. That would teach me for not checking my email daily. I started to scroll down, looking for the jewelers' email address.

"Yes!" There it was. I quickly opened the note:

Thank you for your email, it has relieved the boredom of a slow week. Your pendant is indeed valuable and we believe it might have a very interesting history as well. One of our assistants is following up with the shopkeeper of the store where your parents purchased the jade pendant. In the meantime, here is what we know so far.

The most common color for Jade is light green, but it occurs in many other colors. The most valuable form of Jade, known as "Imperial Jade", is emerald-green. Mottled green and white is also popular. The rarer colors of Jade are yellow, pink, purple (like yours), and black.

Besides its rare color, the intricacy of the carving is also very unusual. Upon closer examination of the photo, a dragon can be seen exquisitely carved into the surface of the jade. This suggests a high degree of craftsmanship, typical of the early Qing Dynasty. As you may know already, in China the dragon is the symbol for Man and is often shown pursuing the ball of perfection. Only a dragon representing the Emperor could ever be depicted holding the ball of perfection in its claws - and that's just what yours is doing!

At this time, we estimate your pendant to be an extremely rare and valuable piece. I will send you another note once we know more.

It was even better than I'd hoped for! In 1644 the Manchu armies had moved south from their homeland to conquer China and establish the Qing, or "pure," dynasty. So something from the Qing Dynasty was really old! I hit the print button so Mom and Dad could read the note.

The rest of my email would have to wait until later; it was time to meet with Adam.

Ten minutes later we were madly cycling down 2nd Avenue to Diefenbaker Park. We wanted to make sure we got there and settled into our positions before dark. I'd brought Dad's binoculars and Adam had a small telescope with a camera attachment.

"So they think your pendant is hundreds of years old?" Adam shouted over the noise of our bikes.

"That's what the jeweler said. I can hardly wait for the next note. My parents were totally amazed as well. They found the pendant in a little shop and thinking back, my mom said the owner almost seemed relieved to have found a buyer for it. For the longest time, they weren't even sure it was real jade since they hadn't paid very much for it."

"That's fantastic!"

As we reached the park, I glanced down to my right. We were up high, overlooking the central pond and weeping willow trees. The resident geese looked like they were settling down in the tall grass for a good night's sleep. Adam and I were both keeping an eye out for 'stray' dogs tonight. We continued up to the end of the street and walked our bikes into the park.

"First thing we should do is set up the telescope," Adam said.

"Do you need a hand with anything?"

"If you could get the camera ready, I'll do the rest."

I pulled Adam's prized camera out of its special case as he set up the telescope. I handled it very carefully since we were at the edge of a steep cliff. The view was spectacular. The north end of the park had an incredible view – probably the best in the whole city. On a clear night, you could see all the way up to the local mountains and down the valley as well. Some of the ski runs were still covered with snow. Directly below us was the highway to the border and just beyond it was farmland that continued out to the Bay. We had a perfect view of the Happy Puppy Obedience School. I helped Adam finish setting up his gear.

"Now comes the worst part of any detective case...the looong wait," Adam exaggerated.

"Let's hope they make their move before it gets too dark," I said, looking through the binoculars. "Anyway, I started telling you about my pendant."

"Why the sudden interest in it?" Adam asked.

"It's hard to explain, Adam. Even though we're both adopted, you know who your birth parents are. Your mom and dad have pictures of your birth parents. Your birth mom sends you a Christmas card every year. I was abandoned and I may never meet my birth parents. For the last couple of weeks, I've been having this re-occurring dream about a mother abandoning her baby in Shanghai and leaving a jade pendant with her as a good luck symbol. I know it's pretty farfetched, but I feel that my pendant may eventually lead me to my own ancestors. That's why I want to find out the history behind it."

Adam nodded. "Yeah. It's easy to forget that I have a family history and I know where I came from. It must be kind of strange not knowing who your birth family was and possibly never being able to find out."

"It's not as big a deal with me as it is with some of the girls on the Sisters of China mailing list. But there is still part of me that would like to find out more one day. Everybody has their dreams and right now this is one of mine."

We went back to watching the kennel. I wanted to ask Adam how he felt about me, but the right moment never came along. We sat quietly through an hour of sheer boredom not saying a word to each other, until...

Adam was the first to notice. "Hey, the kennel door is opening and someone's giving instructions to a brown dog."

"Can you see who it is?"

"No, the door is in the way. All I can see is an arm and part of a red jacket."

"Take some pictures anyway and I'll use the binoculars to see where the dog runs to."

Adam snapped several pictures with his camera. "I'd give

anything to know who owns that hand."

We could see that someone was adjusting the backpack on the dog, but the hood was up on the jacket and we couldn't tell if the person was male or female. The dog was trying to wriggle out of the backpack, but he wasn't a match for Red Jacket. Once the backpack was firmly attached, a hand pointed towards the south and the dog took off.

I jumped up. "The border crossing, Adam! That's where the dog is going. They must be smuggling something across the border in those backpacks. What else could they be doing with these dogs? It's starting to make sense now."

"Can you still see the dog?" Adam asked. "I couldn't keep up with this telescope. I think I got some great photographs though. That dog looked just like one of the dogs I remember seeing on the S.P.C.A. flyers."

"Yep, I've still got him. He's crossing that field below us right now. Can you pull out the flyers and find the one you're thinking of?"

"I think I'd better pack up my camera first. I don't want to leave it here if we're going to try and follow that dog."

As the dog crossed the highway a blue van swerved and narrowly missed running him over.

"He's heading towards the lower end of the park. No time to find the right flyer now. Let's shove everything under those bushes and try to catch him."

We packed up Adam's camera as fast as we could, stowed the rest of the gear under the bushes and raced down the hill on our bikes.

秋玉

16

"There! By the parking lot," Adam pointed at a brown tail disappearing behind a row of parked cars.

The parking lot emptied out to 1st Avenue. Two blocks away, but hidden behind a row of houses, was the border to the United States. We had to catch the dog before he could make it to the border.

"Faster, we're gaining on him," I said, pumping my legs as hard as I could.

We came flying down the hill from 2nd Avenue. I took one side of the pond and Adam took the other. The geese cried out as we madly pedaled by. I decided to head directly towards the kid's play area. Adam was trying to cut him off at the barbecue pits.

I narrowly missed one of the blue, metal drum garbage cans and skidded to a stop by the swings. I dropped my bike and started to run.

The dog saw me coming towards him. He dashed through a yellow tunnel, hopped onto the climbing ramp, cleared two green and red painted logs in one jump and was heading behind the change rooms before I could even open my mouth.

"Adam, he's headed your way, try and stop him!"

Adam was crouching beside a concrete picnic bench. As the dog came out from behind the building, Adam jumped out and tried to grab him.

The dog leapt right over a wooden bench next to Adam and kept on going.

"I'll try to catch him," Adam cried, picking up his bike and frantically cycling after the dog.

I ran back to my bike and then pedaled as hard as I could to keep up.

At the border, the dog went straight through a small opening in the fence and we both watched it disappear into the distance.

"I almost had him," Adam cursed.

"Looks like he's continuing to run south. We can't cross the border into Point Roberts anyway. We'll need our parents to do that. We may as well turn around and head home."

"He was so fast," Adam said. "And did you see how he worked the kid's play area like it was an obstacle course? Someone sure has trained him well."

"He also looked like he was following a scent. He kept sniffing the ground as he was heading towards the border. I think our hunch was right, Adam."

"So now what do we do, Autumn?"

"We've done everything we can do tonight. You'll have to get those pictures developed first thing tomorrow morning. Maybe we'll get a better idea of who was inside the kennel once we see them. I'll talk to my parents when we get home and see if they can drive us down to Point Roberts tomorrow. We really need some concrete evidence before we can talk to the police about what we've seen."

"Any ideas on where we should start looking?" Adam asked.

"Well," I suggested, "we need to find out where the dogs are going before we can solve this mystery."

"We better go back up the hill and pick up our stuff," Adam groaned.

We pushed our bikes most of the way back.

"Boy, I'm just beat," Adam yawned as we arrived home a half-hour later. "Too bad we had to go back to get the equipment. I'll be having a sound sleep tonight."

"Don't go to bed right away, sleepy-head. I'll ask my parents about the trip and hopefully call you in a few minutes."

Luckily, Mom and Dad were both relaxing in the living room. "Mom, Dad, can we go to Point Roberts tomorrow?"

"What for, pumpkin?" Dad asked. "And how come you look so dirty and tired?"

"It's a long story. Do you want the short explanation or do you need the whole thing?"

"Let's start with the shorter version," Dad suggested and Mom nodded her approval.

I told them about the white dog we had seen last Friday, the chat with Mrs. Chandler, the dogs at the kennel, the people Adam had talked to on the phone, and finally what we'd been up to tonight.

"So you see, we need to find out where the dogs are going," I summed up.

"I thought you liked the people at the obedience school," Mom said. "You've been saying all week how wonderful Leslie was."

"And shouldn't you be talking to the police?" Dad added.

"I don't think Leslie knows what's going on," I said to Mom. "And Dad, the police would never believe me. We really don't have any proof yet, do we? That's why we need to go the United

States tomorrow."

Mom and Dad exchanged glances.

"Well, we could go visit the Walkers, if they're not busy," Mom said.

"Who are the Walkers?" I asked.

"Friends of ours from high school," Dad replied. "We haven't seen them in ages."

"Please, can we go see them tomorrow?"

"Sure, I guess we could. Let me give them a call and then we'll see." Mom left the room to use the phone.

"Thanks for believing in me, Dad," I said giving him a big kiss on the cheek.

"You've never steered us wrong before, and you make a very logical case for suspecting the Happy Puppy kennel. I'm proud of what you've done so far."

My ears strained to hear the muffled conversation coming from the kitchen. Clunk, the phone was back on the wall and then footsteps returned down the hallway.

Mom came back into the room. "Okay, everything's all set. The Walkers have invited us all for lunch."

"Thanks, Mom! Can Adam and Watson both come with us?"

"Yes, honey, now that Watson is behaving so well, he can come with us. Adam is always welcome if his parents give us a letter of permission in case we need it crossing the border."

I tried calling but the line was busy, so I ran next door and rang the doorbell.

"Hi, Mrs. B., is Adam still up?"

"Sure, just a second. Adam, Autumn's at the door!"

Adam came down the stairs two at a time. "So what's up?" he asked. "I thought you were going to call?"

"I tried, but the phone was busy."

"I was talking to Vanessa. She called to see if I wanted to go to a movie with her this weekend."

"She didn't waste any time."

"What do you mean by that?" Adam asked in surprise.

"Nothing..."

"C'mon, you've been on Vanessa's case lately. She's a smart girl and easy to talk to. Why are you making such a big deal out of this? I mean, we're just friends."

That's about to change if you're not careful, I thought. "Look, we don't really have time to talk about this right now. My parents have arranged to visit some old high school friends in Point Roberts tomorrow. Ask your Mom if it's okay for you to go."

"Mom!"

"I'm right here, Adam, please don't shout."

"Is it okay if I go to Point Roberts with Autumn and her parents tomorrow?"

"Fine by me," she laughed. "I'll enjoy the day off."

"We'll be leaving at nine-thirty. Bring your bike to our garage before then. I'll be waiting for you." I let out a big yawn. "Oh, I almost forgot. Mrs. B., Mom said something about needing a letter of permission in case the border guards asked."

"I'll have it ready for Adam in the morning, Autumn. Good night."

"Thanks. I guess it is time for bed, have a great sleep Adam!"

I was actually too excited to go to bed right away. Maybe some writing would help me relax...

秋玉
17

Lucky had been carrying messages around Shanghai for several weeks now. Amy was concerned that they were maybe being a little too successful.

"The 'Bamboo Wireless' is onto our activities," Amy stated. "If the Japanese don't know about us yet, they will pretty soon."

Like the ever-present sparrows that hopped in the gutters, public rickshaw pullers hovered in small groups along the curbs, gossiping amicably as they waited for their fares. They were an intrinsic part of the famous Bamboo Wireless. When they delivered their fares they didn't go back to where they had started from, but instead joined the nearest group of pullers, passing on and gathering up all kinds of information. On their endlessly jogging feet, news spread around the International Settlement much faster than by any other medium.

"That's right," added Soo-Lin. "I've heard people talking about Lucky. Many people can now spot him by sight."

"Well, we're committed to sending at least one more message," Qiu said. "We can't back out now. It's my turn to meet our American friend at the Hongkew Market and send out Lucky with the note. Wish me luck!"

"Be careful, Qiu Yu," they both said, giving her fierce bear hugs.

"I'll see you back at the statue in no time," Qiu bragged with little conviction in her voice. She was more nervous than she had ever been before. Her legs were shaking and her breakfast was trying to crawl back up her throat.

The Hongkew Market was located at the corner of Boone and Woosung Roads, right in the heart of Japanese territory. Lucky had been trained to sneak along in the shadows when they went to the drop off. Qiu was dressed like a farmer's daughter, including a big sack of bok choy that she was supposedly taking to her honorable uncle's stall. She had a forged pass to get through any checkpoints. No one questioned her and Qiu safely made it to the market. Lucky was waiting behind a big tank of golden-scaled fish.

Qiu gave him a rub under the chin and around his ears. "Good boy, Lucky. So far so good."

Hongkew Market drew hundreds of fishermen, farmers and butchers bringing in produce they hoped to sell within a few hours of their arriving. You could purchase everything from live duck to lobster. There were fruits and vegetables stacked in miniature mountains, waiting to be distributed among the stalls. In huge tubs, thousands of "walkee-walkee" fish gazed with indifferent eyes at the descending cleaver.

Qiu quickly glanced around. Even though she couldn't see anything to make her suspicious, the hairs on the back of her neck were standing on end. She sensed that she and Lucky were being watched. Qiu had positioned herself with a full view down one of the long aisles. She didn't recognize Jimmy until he was standing right beside her.

"That's the best disguise yet," Qiu said out of the side of her mouth.

"Missee wanchee one piece rickshaw?" he jokingly replied. "Guess I must look just like a rickshaw coolie if I had you fooled."

"It's definitely a convincing costume. Good thing too, Amy's worried that the Japanese might be on to us. You probably shouldn't be seen with me for too much longer. Got the messages?" she asked, quickly getting down to business. Qiu was feeling nervous again. This time she was convinced they were being watched.

"Sure thing, Qiu. Here you go, and good luck."

Jimmy quickly faded into the crowd. Qiu turned to Lucky and tied the package with Jimmy's messages to his collar.

"Good boy, Lucky, you know the routine..."

Two sets of strong hands suddenly grabbed her from behind. Qiu turned and saw the sleeve of a Japanese soldier! She bent forward and drove her heel behind her into the soldier's shin with all her weight. Qiu managed to break free and quickly tied her jade pendant onto Jimmy's package.

"Run Lucky, go get help!" she shouted, shooing him away with her right foot. One of the soldiers tried to snatch him up, but Lucky dodged to the left and then took off into the market, his legs gathering speed as he darted through the crowd forming around Qiu and the soldiers.

The two soldiers dragged Qiu kicking and screaming towards the back of the market. Auntie Shu-Shu was going to love hearing about this.

"I'm the daughter of a rich and powerful farmer," she cried out. "Someone help me! My father will shower you with gifts."

Her calls for help weren't working. People were staring, but no one reacted to Qiu's offer. She suddenly remembered that this time she was dressed as a poor farmer's daughter. "No wonder I'm not getting any help!"

The soldiers opened a door in the side of a narrow alley. They pushed Qiu up a flight of filthy stairs to a small office overlooking the market. One of the soldiers opened the door, while the other roughly pushed her through. Then they closed the door behind them, leaving Qiu in the room with its sole occupant.

Sitting at an old wooden desk was a Japanese soldier, obviously an officer by the crispness of his uniform and the braiding on his lapels.

"Please sit down, young lady," he said in perfect Oxford English, waving towards a rickety chair in front of his desk. "My name is Lieutenant Umoto. I am going to ask you a few simple questions."

Qiu pretended that she couldn't understand him.

"Come now Qiu Yu, we know all about you and your friends. We only want to know what was in those packages you've been transporting to the Chinese Army."

Qiu bit her tongue and continued to act dumb.

"Well, if you won't talk, let me tell you a little story that may change your mind. There has been friction between the Japanese and the Chinese since the war of 1894. Japanese military operations in Manchuria last year intensified the anti-Japanese feeling in China. This past January, five Japanese monks started singing Japanese patriotic songs in a Chinese factory here in Shanghai. They were celebrating Japan's success in taking over Manchuria and the establishment of Manchukuo, with Henry Pu-yi, deposed Emperor of China, as Emperor. This provoked rioting during which one of the monks was lynched."

Lieutenant Umoto paused for a moment and then smiled at Qiu. "In reprisal, the Japanese landed 1,200 marines and ordered the Chinese Nationalist garrison commander, General Cai Tingkai, to withdraw his Nineteenth Route Army. He refused, and we attacked."

Qiu started to squirm in her seat. The Lieutenant switched tactics and tried a compliment.

"For 34 days the Chinese have bravely resisted. The information that you and your friends have been smuggling to the Chinese Army has only prolonged things. In the last month, 18,000 people have been killed or gone missing. This has been a most unnecessary waste of human life."

"It's your fault that people have died," Qiu blurted out. "This is China. You and your Japanese friends are not wanted here!"

The lieutenant stood up and raised his arm to strike her. A knock on the door stayed his hand. Instead, he walked over and opened the door. There was a brief heated conversation in Japanese followed by excited backslapping. Lieutenant Umoto turned back to face Qiu.

"You can go, Qiu Yu, but do not think that we are through with you. I will remember the espionage work you were involved with and next time I will not be so lenient."

"What, just like that?" Qiu asked, snapping her fingers in the air.

"The Chinese Nineteenth Route Army has retreated from the Chapei district. We have won. This little conflict is over."

"It's not over by a long shot," Qiu said with as much pride as she could muster. She ran down the stairs, right into Sergei's arms. Lucky had gone straight to Amy and Soo-Lin. When they saw her pendant, they knew that she was in trouble. Together they had found Sergei and followed Lucky back to the market.

Qiu hugged her friends. "We've lost."

"We will not speak of winning or losing," Sergei said calmly.

"Each side does what they must. Today we should celebrate that we fought the battle with bravery and integrity. Let's go have a fine meal at the Willow Pattern Tea House, my treat."

Qiu needed to change so they agreed to meet in one hour at the entrance to the 'zig-zag' bridges. The Willow Pattern Tea House was supposed to be the original tea house on the blue porcelain "willow pattern" plates. The Tea House was built on stone pillars in a pool, approached by a zig-zag of bridges to keep the demons away. Around the pool there was a kaleidoscopic glimpse of Chinese life. Dentists, doctors, toy vendors, cooks and jugglers carried on their trades in the open with the admiring spectators freely offering advice. Near the pool there were several bird markets with gorgeous collections.

"Can Lucky come, too?" Soo-Lin asked.

"Of course he can. He is, after all, the guest of honour!" Amy proudly stated.

Sergei nodded his head in consent.

On the way home Qiu thought of the hot tea and mountains of steaming rice she would consume. She would listen to the clack, clack of Mahjong tiles as they stood on the zig-zag bridge watching the turtles in the green, stagnant water. Later, she would wander around the bird market and listen to the songs of the oriole. Yes, they had done their part to help China, and deserved a party. Shanghai, being the city that it was, would be back to normal in a week or two.

* * *

I thought of all the history books I'd read. "Normal, that is, until the next time, when the Japanese would invade for real..."

秋玉

18

I woke up early to the smell of blackberry pancakes cooking on the griddle.

"Come on, Watson, time to get some breakfast. We have a big day ahead of us." I dug out some comfortable clothes for our exploration of Point Roberts and quickly changed.

After breakfast, Dad strapped our bikes onto the back of the Land Rover.

"So the deal is," Dad began, "you two have to stay close by and be ready to leave when we're done."

I crossed my fingers behind my back and glanced at Adam. "We promise," I said.

Dad drove us to the mall to drop off Adam's roll of film and then we headed to the border. When we got there, two of the three booths were open. When it was our turn, the Customs Officer leaned through the window of his booth, looked in our car and asked, "Are you all Canadian citizens?"

"Yes we are," Dad answered.

"Purpose of your visit?"

"Just visiting some friends for lunch and then doing a little sight-seeing."

The officer gave Dad an x-ray vision look and then curtly dismissed us. "Okay, please proceed."

There are two main populated areas in Point Roberts. One is the southern tip of the peninsula, and the other is on the east shore, close to the border. Lucky for us, the Walkers lived in the south. Because of the route the dog was taking and the fact that the American obedience school was also in that direction, Adam and I knew it was the southern community that we really needed to check out.

"I didn't realize it was so much like the countryside down here," I commented. "We're really not very far from the city."

"Yeah, so far it's been mostly brush land and barbed wire fences," Adam added.

The first sign of civilization was the Sunset Point Resort trailer park. It was a bunch of rickety old trailers, tired looking trees, and lots of people sitting out in their yards. It would be a good place to ask about the dogs. I made a mental note to go there first.

Dad turned left onto Marine Road. "Almost there," he said.

Smoke from yard fires was filling the air and billowing across the road. We drove through the smoke and immediately on our right there was a sign saying 'Lighthouse Marine Park.' Adam whispered to me that this was another possible place to scope out.

We came around a tight curve and suddenly in front of us was a man-made inlet, surrounded by expensive looking houses. It looked like something from a Florida tourist magazine, with water access to a marina and big, luxurious homes. Adam and I must have both dropped our jaws at the same time.

"We're here," Mom said. "Please close your mouths before you get out of the car."

"They live here?" I stammered.

"Just because we don't live in a castle doesn't mean we might not have friends that do," Mom quipped.

We all piled out of the Land Rover and Dad removed our bikes.

"Once we've introduced you to the Walkers, you can go do your investigating."

"But remember, we want you back here for lunch by twelve o'clock sharp," Mom added.

"Okay," we both chimed in.

The Walkers' house was probably the most incredible place I had ever seen. From the big country porch that wrapped around the whole front of the house to the red cedar deck out back, it was absolutely beautiful. We waited on the porch while Mom rang the doorbell.

"I think you'll like the Walkers," Mom said. "They are very nice people."

The door opened and a tall, elegant-looking woman stepped out. She gave Mom a big hug. "It's great to see you again, Janet. And John, you're looking good."

"Thanks, Diane," Dad said. "And you remember Autumn, don't you? I think she's grown a bit, though, since the last time you saw her."

"You've become a very stunning young woman," she said.

My face turned red. "This is my friend Adam," I managed to blurt out.

She put out her hand and smiled at Adam. "Glad to meet you, Adam."

Dad explained that Adam and I wanted to go exploring before lunch.

"Anywhere in particular?" she asked.

"We thought we might start with the trailer park we passed on the way here," Adam said.

"You'll want to talk to Mrs. Lee, then."

"Why?" I asked.

"She's a bit eccentric, but she seems to know most of the things that go on around here."

Dad was curious. "Eccentric?"

"They'll find out what I mean. Well, you two kids go enjoy yourselves," said Mrs. Walker. "Come back with some good appetites!"

"Thanks, you bet we will," I replied.

Adam reached the end of the driveway first. "Where to?"

"The trailer park and then we'll go check out the obedience school. Maybe Mrs. Lee can give us some good clues to follow."

We cycled back to the Sunset Point Resort trailer park on Gulf Road. Watson ran along beside us, stopping to check out interesting smells and then dashing full out to catch up again.

I was hoping that Mrs. Lee might have spotted one of our dogs. We reached the trailer park in no time and laid down our bikes at the first trailer we came to. A small white sign on the picket fence said 'Lee.' I went over and knocked on the door.

We could hear some shuffling about. "Who's there?" a sleepy voice called out from inside the trailer.

"My name is Autumn. My friend Adam and I are looking for a missing dog. Can we ask you some questions?" I yelled back through the door.

"I'm not deaf, you know. You don't have to shout. I'll be there in a minute."

The door opened and the oldest Chinese woman I'd ever seen was standing in front of us. She had tissue paper skin and shocking white hair. She sized us up for a minute, then looked at me and asked in Chinese, "How come you do not greet me properly?"

"Ni hao ma," I said.

"Oh my! I'm greeted by a banana, yellow on the outside, white on the inside."

"Excuse me," I responded in Mandarin. "I find that term offensive. It's not polite to call a guest to your house by a name like that."

That made her eyes open wide. "Ooh, aren't we the sassy one. I'm sorry if I offended you, but I wanted to see what you were really made of."

"I am Chinese," I stated firmly. "I was born in China and lived there the first year of my life."

"That doesn't make you Chinese, young lady. Inside you are white. You do not have the culture and upbringing that a real Chinese like myself has."

I stepped closer to the door and planted my feet.

"You don't know that, and it hurts when you make that assumption. I celebrate all of the Chinese festivals, I'm almost fluent in Mandarin, I can write my Chinese characters, and I've been doing t'ai chi since I was a little girl."

I didn't want to tell her that my parents sometimes went a little overboard with the Chinese culture and history thing. When I was younger, I really didn't have much of a choice in the matter. Now I did it because I liked it. And so we stood in her doorway, neither one of us willing to back down.

Luckily I had taught Adam some basic Chinese and he had a formed a pretty good idea about what we'd been saying to each other.

"Can we start over again? We're sorry if we've disturbed you. My name is Adam and this is my friend Autumn. We're trying to find some dogs that have gone missing in the Tsawwassen area."

"My name is Mrs. Lee and welcome to my humble home. But I

see you already have a dog, so why do you need another one?" she said with a big, toothy grin.

"We're looking for some special dogs," Adam continued. "They would have been running towards the south with small packs on their backs."

"Now that is very interesting," she said and then just stopped and smiled at us.

Eccentric? She was exasperating! "If you know anything that could help us out, we would be very thankful," I joined in.

"Would you be thankful enough to come and visit me again? I'm sorry if I offended you. I get very lonely and am unaccustomed to greeting guests in my home now that all of my friends and most of my family have gone to meet their ancestors."

"I'm also sorry that we got off to a bad start. I promise that I'll ask my parents later today about coming back to see you."

Mrs. Lee visibly relaxed. "Okay, then. I take a walk along the beach in the park every evening. I've seen dogs with packs on at least five occasions in the past month. It was very peculiar, that's why I remember it so well. You should go visit the park and ask the people who work there. They've seen the dogs, too."

Adam and I exchanged excited glances.

"Thank you. Mrs. Lee, you've been a big help," I said.

I was turning to leave when her hand darted out and grabbed my jade pendant. "Oh my, oh my," she said. "This is very interesting, very interesting indeed. We will definitely be meeting again."

Mrs. Lee then closed the door to her trailer and was gone. Somehow I felt that she was right about us meeting again.

Adam shook his head. "That was sure weird."

"I'm glad we talked to her, though. There is something oddly familiar about her. Thanks for breaking the ice, Adam. We probably would have never learned about the dogs if you hadn't spoken up. I think we better check out the beach next, instead of the obedience school. We can come back to visit the school after lunch."

"Sounds good to me."

"Come on, Watson, off we go."

It only took us a couple of minutes to get back to Lighthouse Marine Park.

"Cool!" exclaimed Adam. "What a great view."

"I wish we could live here," I sighed. "Look at how much fun Watson is having. I think the fresh air is good for him."

The beach was covered in all kinds of driftwood. Watson leapt from log to log like a wild maniac. Then he darted into the surf and came out soaking wet. Just down the beach we could see a kid's playground with a pirate tower, swings, a slide, and little covered buildings for picnics. There was a group of young children swarming all over the tower.

"Let's ask those kids on the pirate tower if they've seen any dogs with backpacks on," I said.

We were walking along pushing our bikes through the sand when Watson started to bark like crazy.

"I think he's picked up a scent trail," Adam said excitedly.

"What it is, boy?" I called.

"Look!" cried Adam. "I don't believe it. Another dog with a backpack is running this way!"

I fingered my pendant and said a silent thank-you to Mrs. Lee. "We can't lose him this time. You go back to the road and follow from there. Watson and I will try to keep up along the beach."

Adam wished us good luck, and Watson and I took off after the dog. The chase was on!

秋玉

19

This time the dog we were chasing was a blonde lab or retriever cross. The green backpack it wore swayed from side to side.

"I'll never be able to keep up in this soft sand," I cursed to myself. Why did I offer to stay on the beach? Watson would have to keep an eye on the dog while I dragged my bike over a wall of driftwood to the firmer sand near the water; there was no easy path in sight. I hoisted my bicycle onto my right shoulder and climbed as fast as I could. I was almost over the pile of logs when I stepped on a wobbly stump and slipped.

"Ouch! Oh, that smarts."

I managed to catch my balance, but only after the pedal of my bike scraped down my thigh. There were only a few drops of blood, but it hurt like crazy.

"Ooof, I'm coming Watson!"

The tide was out and the firm wet sand was perfect for cycling on. I ignored the pain in my leg by concentrating on the rapidly disappearing dog ahead. The few glimpses I had of the beach made it difficult to concentrate on the chase at hand. The clear blue water and the small tidal pools teeming with tiny fish and other creatures made me silently wish I had more time to enjoy the beach, instead of madly racing past everything. We'd have to come back.

The beach was curving to the east. I lost sight of both Watson and the blonde dog. I hadn't realized it, but Watson must have been keeping an eye on me as well as the dog. He came into view again, doing crazy circles in the sand waiting for me.

"Woof, woof, woof," Watson barked.

"Thanks for waiting, what a good boy you are!" I puffed and off we went again.

I lost sight of the dog when we reached a jumble of large boulders and once again Watson waited for me to catch up. I was thankful that Adam and I had done the scent training with Watson. I fleetingly thought about how Adam was doing. I couldn't see the road from here on the beach. But I would bet he was having an easier time of it than I was.

The dog seemed to be heading towards the marina behind the Walker's place. The beach must be an easier and less conspicuous route for the dogs to take. If this dog was indeed heading for the marina it was going to be very difficult for me to find him among the hundreds of tall masts visible from the beach.

I'd lost Watson yet again when the beach dead-ended at a breakwater jutting out from the shore. I turned to see if there was a way up to the road and there was Adam wildly pointing his arms toward the boats in the marina.

"I have the dog in sight!" he yelled down at me.

"Go ahead without me," I shouted back. "I'll find you."

I got off my bike to carry it back over the stacks of driftwood that formed a solid barrier surrounding the entire beach. When I finally reached the road, Watson was sitting in the grass waiting for me.

"Let me catch my breath, Watson," I sighed. I was aching everywhere. "Okay boy, show me where Adam went. Go find Adam."

Watson took off straight to the marina. Every few seconds he would glance behind to make sure I was still there.

"I'm trying Watson, I'm really trying." I was actually thinking about packing it in. I was feeling awfully light-headed and woozy.

Adam had stopped and was waiting by the marina entrance. I practically ran him over I was concentrating so hard on the road beneath my tires.

"Watch it," Adam cried.

I snapped out of it in time to slam on my brakes. When I looked up at Adam, I started to laugh hysterically.

"It's not funny, Autumn."

"What happened? You look like a slime monster from an old horror movie."

"Every once in a while I caught a glimpse of you and Watson on the beach so I knew where you were. It was pretty easy for me to keep up, but about two miles back there was an old tractor blocking my way. I tried to go around it, but just when I thought I was okay, I slipped into the muck-filled ditch that runs along the side of the road."

"Are you okay?"

"Beside smelling bad, I'll be all right. How about you? There's a lot of blood on your leg!"

I looked down at my leg and almost fainted. The scrape on my thigh from the bike pedal was actually a gash and the blood must have been oozing down my leg for most of the chase. No wonder I was feeling so weak. Mixed with the sand and water that flew up as I was cycling, it was an ugly red mess. Lucky for me, the bleeding had finally stopped.

"We must look just awful."

"Nothing a hot bath won't fix. Your parents aren't going to be too happy with us, though."

"We can't worry about them yet. What about the dog, where did it go?"

"I saw the ship it went onto, and wait until you see it! I think Watson has gone over to stand guard for us."

"Thanks," I sighed. "What would I do without you, Adam?"

I think Adam looked pleased under the green slime, but it was hard to tell.

Now that I'd had a little break, I was feeling much better.

"Let's go," I said, straightening my shoulders.

"This way," Adam said, leading the way. "We can walk our bikes over to the dock."

Watson was sitting very still staring at an enormous boat. The name painted on the side was 'After Eight' and the ship was the same colour as the box of chocolates.

"It looks like it's over a hundred feet long!"

Adam nodded his head in agreement. "Someone sure has a ton of money."

We hid our bikes behind a rusting storage container and began casually walking towards the 'After Eight.'

"I didn't see anyone on the deck when the dog ran up," Adam whispered.

"Maybe no one is there right now. Let's sneak on board and take a look around."

"I don't think that's a good idea, Autumn."

"We have Watson to protect us. Come on, we haven't come this far to back out now."

"I'll go first then." Adam crept up the gangplank and Watson and I followed right behind. The ship was eerily quiet. The door to the main cabin was open. Adam looked back at me, winked and then stepped inside. Watson looked happy and was wagging his tail. Must be safe enough...

I had just stepped over the threshold when I fleetingly saw a blond-haired shadow move on my left. I blacked out just as I landed on Adam, who was slumped down on the carpet in front of me...

秋玉

20

"Autumn. Wake up, Autumn." It was Adam's voice coming from far way.

Oooh, my head felt like I'd been hit by a truck. I slowly opened my eyes to see Adam, Eddie from the kennel, and Watson all staring down at me.

"Welcome back," Adam smiled. Watson gently licked my face.

"I guess we've been captured?" I ventured. The room we were in was amazing. Beautifully crafted wood, marble, gold, stainless steel, custom wool carpets and antique leather surrounded us.

Adam was all cleaned up and somebody had washed my leg and dressed my wound.

"There's an en-suite bathroom with a shower," he said. "I feel much better now that most of the slime is gone."

Eddie spoke up. "We're being detained on Frank Dixon's private yacht. You've been unconscious for over an hour. Adam and I were beginning to wonder whether you might have received a concussion from the blow to your head."

"Beside having a splitting headache, I think everything's still working. I probably just needed some sleep." I stretched all of my muscles to make sure. "But what are you doing here? You were one of my prime suspects up until thirty seconds ... uh, make that an hour ago."

"You were right to think I was involved," Eddie replied. "We seem to have some time on our hands so I'll explain what happened. When the Happy Puppy opened for business, I was hired on to run the kennel. I never actually met Mr. Dixon's brother, the supposed owner. It was Frank Dixon and his wife who hired me. You've probably seen her in the front office."

"Ms. Greasy Hair!"

Eddie chuckled. "A very apt description of her, Autumn. Anyway, everything was going along great until I made the mistake of coming to work with a bad headache. I accidentally gave the wrong medication to one of the dogs we were looking after. Frank Dixon somehow found out and threatened to have me fired unless I helped him with a special job. He told me I would find it very lucrative if everything went smoothly. I was just out of jail and working at the kennel was my first real job in a long time. What could I do? Frank was stealing dogs, and he needed Leslie and I..."

"Leslie," I spluttered. "No way!"

"Leslie is Frank Dixon's niece. She's in it up to her eyeballs, I'm afraid. Heck, most of the tracking ideas and dognapping victims came from her. Anyway, Frank needed Leslie and I to train the dogs to carry..."

"Diamonds?" Adam guessed, warming up to the game.

"Well done," I congratulated him.

"I just remembered that newspaper article we read in the library. It suddenly all made sense."

"Kids these days," Eddie laughed. "So what is there left to explain?"

"What are they going to do with us?" I asked.

"Who owned the little white dog that we chased through the park?" This bulldog determination to see something through was a new side of Adam that I liked.

"I'll start with Adam's question since I know the answer to it. We used Mr. Dixon's white Miniature Spitz several times to make the deliveries. 'Sir Henry' is getting pretty old and he followed the wrong scent trail the day you saw him. Mr. Dixon picked him up at the other side of the park using a dog whistle."

"'Sir Henry'," Adam smiled. "What a funny name for a dog."

"He was a very famous dog in his day," Eddie responded. "He earned a roomful of trophies for excellence in tracking trials. He was a champion of champions."

"As for your question, Autumn, I don't think it looks too good for us. I told Mr. Dixon I wanted out. I couldn't sleep at nights, I was worrying so much. Next thing I knew, I woke up here. There's an awful lot of money at stake. I wouldn't give us good odds at getting out of here alive. This is a huge ship, and we're about as far down inside it as you can go."

"I have an idea, if you're willing to try it," I said.

"I'd give pretty much any suggestion a try right now. Let's hear it." Adam nodded his head in agreement with Eddie.

"I'll tie my jade pendant to Watson's collar. We can break the porthole glass and push him through. He'll swim to shore, find my parents and bring back help."

Adam had a look of serious disbelief on his face. "No way! Watson may be smart, but he's not Lassie, you know."

"Don't be hasty, Adam," Eddie said. "Watson is a very smart dog. With the right commands, he might be able to pull this off. I think Autumn's idea is an excellent one. Pass me your pendant, Autumn, and I'll fasten it to Watson's collar."

Eddie tied the pendant to Watson's collar and then sat quietly with him repeating our rescue instructions.

"Go find Mom, go find Dad, bring them here. Go find Mom, go find Dad, bring them back to us..."

"We need something to break the porthole glass," Adam whispered to me. "Let's take a look around."

Adam rummaged through the closets and I checked the chest of drawers, but this luxurious stateroom was completely empty of anything useful.

Eddie finished with Watson. "I think our only choice is to break a leg off of that chair and use it to smash the glass."

"Won't that be pretty noisy?" Adam commented.

"Yes, it will. We'll have to move very fast to make sure we get Watson out of the porthole before someone comes down to see what's going on. Ready?"

Adam and I both nodded our heads.

Eddie picked up the chair and swung it into the steel wall. Crash! Nothing happened! He swung it again even harder. This time a chair leg broke off in his hand. Without hesitation, he drove it into the porthole glass. Thump, thump. We could hear footsteps running up above. Smash. Finally the window broke and the pieces went flying out over the water. Eddie cleaned out the little bits of glass still in the frame and then picked up Watson. The footsteps were coming down the hallway.

"Hurry, Eddie," I cried.

"Good boy, Watson," Eddie said calmly. "This is going to be a tight fit. Remember, bring back Mom, bring back Dad." And with that, Eddie shoved Watson through the porthole. We rushed to look out the window. Down he went. Plop! He disappeared beneath the surface of the murky water. 2, 3, 4, 5 seconds and then he reappeared swimming towards the shore.

"Go, Watson, go," I silently prayed.

The door was flung open and Mr. Dixon took a quick look around. He turned a nasty shade of red when he saw the broken porthole and figured out that Watson was now missing.

Leslie was right behind him. She gave us a withering look. "Now you've gone and done it!"

"Tell the crew to get under way immediately," Mr. Dixon snarled at her. Leslie ran out the door. "You three have just made up my mind for me," he said turning back to us. A gun had appeared in his hand. "There was going to be one more delivery tonight, but we'll have to leave now and dump you three overboard once we're at sea."

The engines roared into life and the ship started to strain at its moorings. After a few minutes, Leslie returned.

"All set, Uncle Frank. We'll be going shortly."

We needed to stall for time. I figured we'd better keep them talking.

"How many diamonds did you manage to smuggle?" I asked. By the look on both their faces, I knew I'd gotten it right.

"How the..." Mr. Dixon stammered.

"You're too smart for you're own good," Leslie spat out. "I'm glad I knocked you unconscious."

The ship rocked back and forth several times and then accelerated away from the dock. Leslie and Mr. Dixon visibly relaxed once the ship was underway.

"It was so obvious," I began. "We read the article in the local paper announcing the opening of the Happy Puppy Obedience School. It said that the owner's brother, that's you Mr. Dixon, had helped finance the school. The paper also said that you ran a big diamond mine up north. When we followed one of your dogs to the border, we put it all together. The final thing we needed was to know where the dogs were going. That was the proof we were missing before we could go to the police."

"How come you had to steal so many dogs?" Adam asked, looking sideways at me as he said it. I felt much better knowing that he was in this, too.

"It was too difficult to train the dogs to follow the scent trail in both directions," Mr. Dixon began. "We had thirty-five trips to make..."

I quickly did some mental math – what a lot of diamonds!

"...and my two dogs weren't going to be enough to transfer all of the diamonds in the month I had while my brother and his wife were on vacation. Never in my wildest dreams did I think a couple of nosy kids would stumble onto our secret."

"It was all because of your little white dog limping through the park," Adam replied. "If we hadn't tried to find the dog's owner, we would have never discovered what you were up to. It only took a few phone calls to people who had recently lost a dog to uncover the pattern. It was enough to make us suspicious of the Happy Puppy School and its staff. What's ironic is that you were the dog's owner all along. I think that's pretty funny, don't you?"

We must have cleared the harbour. The ship was steadily accelerating to full speed and I could no longer see land through the porthole. Mr. Dixon was nervously fingering his gun. The ship suddenly veered to the left. Through the porthole we could hear a powerful ship coming after us. Ms. Greasy Hair showed up in the doorway and frantically whispered to Leslie and her husband.

"Blah, blah, blah, Coast Guard, blah, blah."

All right, Watson! Mr. Dixon glared at us and then all three of them left the room, locking the door behind them.

秋玉

21

"Everything is going to be okay, we're saved," Adam cheered.

"Not so fast," Eddie interrupted. "Smuggling is bad enough, but kidnapping is extremely serious. Mr. Dixon can't afford to have us discovered on his ship if it gets stopped. We're not out of this yet. We'll need a plan for when they come back."

"If we could only overpower Mr. Dixon and get his gun," Adam began. "Wait a minute! I've just had an idea. Here's what I'm thinking..."

We gathered around Adam as he went over his plan. When Adam was finished, Eddie stood up and said, "You're sure you want to do that, Adam? Well, if we get the timing right, it should work."

Adam smiled and then went into the bathroom to prepare for his role.

"How are you holding up, Autumn?" Eddie asked. "You look as frightened as I feel."

Great. I was looking to Eddie for strength and he was scared too. "Of course I'm frightened. I've never been this close to a gun before, especially in the hands of someone who wants to kill me.

But I'm really glad that you and Adam are here. The three of us have made a pretty good team so far."

"Yeah, we have," Eddie smiled. "I was on the wrong side for too long. I wish I'd never become involved with Mr. Dixon and his plans. I know the police will probably arrest me for my part in his smuggling operation, even though I was forced into it."

"Who's to say that Mr. Dixon didn't set up that whole incident with the wrong medicine just to entrap you? You were blackmailed into working with them, after all. That's got to count for something with the police."

Adam came back into the room. "Nice work, Adam. You look just awful," I said admiringly.

Adam wiped some soap from the corner of his mouth. "I hope they get down here soon, I'd hate to have to do this again."

The ship had continued to swerve in different directions. I tried to see what was happening by poking my head through the porthole and immediately received a face full of seawater. "Brrrr, that's cold. It is the Coast Guard, and they're closing the gap fast!"

There were footsteps coming down the hallway again. The door opened and Mr. Dixon waved at us with his gun. "Time for a short swim," he said motioning towards the doorway.

Adam immediately put his plan into action. His idea had been to make himself sick and then distract Mr. Dixon by throwing up.

"Me one piece sickee, sickee. Catchee doctor, chop chop," Adam threw up on the carpet. He then moaned and groaned his way across the floor using Pidgin-English until he was lying on the carpet right in front of an astonished Mr. Dixon. Adam rolled over and threw up again, just missing Mr. Dixon's shiny shoes.

"Get up, boy, and quit talking so funny. You won't care soon enough anyway," he threatened.

Adam began to slowly rise, but halfway up he dove with all of his weight at Mr. Dixon's kneecaps. On cue, Eddie lunged for the gun and I whacked Mr. Dixon over the head with the chair leg.

As he crumpled to the ground, the key to our prison fell out of Mr. Dixon's left hand. Eddie scooped up the key and with gun in hand, led the way out of our temporary prison cell. As we locked the door behind us, Mr. Dixon became a prisoner on his own yacht!

It was eerily quiet out in the hallway.

Adam leaned back against the wall. "What if he wakes up?" he whispered.

"He'll be out for a while, Autumn took care of that. It was a good, solid hit she planted on his head."

"Thanks!" I grinned.

"Sounds like we might be the only ones down here."

"They're probably all top-side watching the chase. Plus, I bet no one else was willing to be an accessory to murder. I'm sure they were all very happy to let Mr. Dixon do it on his own."

Eddie headed towards the back of the ship.

Adam couldn't contain himself. "This ship really is something! Look, they actually have two washers and two dryers in the laundry room. And check out this kitchen. That fridge could hold enough food for weeks at sea!"

When we reached the central lobby, Eddie drew out the gun and took the lead up the stairs to the main deck.

There was a large dining room at the top of the stairs. There was a huge wall mural and a table that looked big enough to seat twelve adults comfortably. Just past the dining room was an enormous living room with wall-to-wall bookshelves.

"Uh, oh," Adam cried out, then quickly covered his mouth.

"What?" Eddie asked, looking around nervously.

"Look at all the books! Now we'll never get Autumn out of

here."

Eddie let out a sigh of relief and I punched Adam in the arm. There was still no one in sight.

"We better go up to the sun deck to see what's going on," Eddie said.

As we slowly crept up the final stairway, the ship started to slow down and the engines grew quiet. Eddie peered over the edge of the top stair.

"All clear," he called down to us. "The cavalry is here!"

Up on the deck, the Coast Guard had things under control. Leslie and Ms. Greasy Hair were already in handcuffs. The rest of the crew huddled together, overseen by several watchful Coast Guard soldiers with machine guns.

Eddie handed Mr. Dixon's gun and the key to the cabin to the nearest Coast Guard officer. He also let him know where Mr. Dixon could be found. We were escorted to a small lounge overlooking the deck below. The Coast Guard crew fired up the engines and headed the ship back to the shore.

"Well, Adam..."

"Well, Autumn..." We both started to giggle hysterically from relief.

"I can't believe how close we came to being thrown overboard. Without your diversion we might be dead by now."

Adam blushed. "You're my best friend, Autumn. I couldn't let anything bad happen to you."

I suddenly had this urge to lean over and give Adam a big hug.

But Adam jumped up and ran to the window. "Hey, I can see the marina..."

Eddie was sitting quietly looking through a book on dogs. "Watcha looking at?" I asked, temporarily giving up on Adam.

"It's called the 'Great Big Book of Dog Breeds and Breeders' and here on page 57 is a picture of Mr. Dixon and Sir Henry," he replied.

"Wait a minute," I gasped. "I've seen that book before. I was in the library last week and decided I didn't have time to look through it. If only I had, we would have been able to solve this mystery and avoid all this trouble!"

Adam came back to take a look. "That's the book Vanessa was telling me about! It really is the little white dog we chased in the park! That's amazing."

Adam and I began laughing so hard we couldn't stop. Eddie hesitated for a moment, and then joined us with a deep belly laugh. Good thing no one else could hear us, they'd probably have thought we'd all gone crazy.

秋玉

22

The yacht slowly approached the dock. There was a big crowd of people waiting for us. I could see Mom, Dad, the Walkers, and Watson with his tail proudly thumping the wooden planks of the dock. Mrs. Lee was standing next to Mom.

The local police boarded the ship to collect Mr. Dixon and the rest of his gang.

"We were so worried when lunchtime went by, and then only Watson showed up," Mom gushed, with tears of relief rolling down her face.

"Are you okay?" Dad asked, giving me a fierce hug. He dug into his pocket and pulled out my pendant.

"Thanks, Baba. I'm fine, honest."

"You look terrible. What happened to your leg?" Mom asked.

"It's nothing that a hot bath and a good night's sleep won't fix," I smiled.

"And how about you, Adam? You look like you've been sick."

"It's a long story. I'm sure Autumn can tell it better than I can," Adam replied, weaseling out of an explanation.

"Mrs. Lee, I was very surprised when I saw you waiting here,"

I said, bowing to her.

"Your mother and I have been talking. When I was a young girl in China I had a daughter that I was forced to abandon on the streets of Shanghai. I think we can help each other with the demons that live in our dreams."

"You know about my dream? I started writing it down and now it's turned into a whole story. No one else has read it besides me, though," I confided.

"I'm an old woman, Autumn Jade. I know about many things, including, I think, the history behind your jade pendant."

A police officer interrupted our conversation. "Excuse me, young lady, there are two police detectives who would like to talk to you and your friend. Once they've taken your statements, you'll be free to go home."

"Okay, we'll be there in a minute. Mom, can Mrs. Lee come to stay with us for a while?"

Mom and Mrs. Lee exchanged a strange look. "She and I will discuss it while you're giving your statement," she replied.

We gave the detectives the full story of our adventure, ending with the Coast Guard chase and our escape from Mr. Dixon. We were interrupted several times by police officers coming over to talk excitedly to the two detectives.

After what seemed like an hour of questions, the older detective finally wrapped things up. "That's quite a story, young lady. If you had come to me yesterday with such a tale I would have laughed you out of my office. As it is, you and your friend have uncovered a major smuggling operation that was happening right under our noses. While we've been talking, our men have recovered the diamonds. They were sewn into the sides of several life jackets on the ship. It also turns out that the people living on the 'C'est Si Bon', that Catamaran putting up the sail over there, have a dog that they thought was going crazy. It would bark at all hours of the day and night, staring only at Mr. Dixon's yacht. They kept watch and eventually saw several of the dogs with backpacks running onto the ship. They thought of calling the police, but weren't sure what to say."

We were interrupted one more time by a police officer waving a cell phone at the detectives. The older detective went over to take the call.

"Good news," he said when he returned. "Office Davis has just informed me that the owner of the dog you chased this morning is already on her way, so it's a happy ending all around. We'll probably need to contact you again, but for now you can go home for a well-deserved rest. Good work, you two. Well done!"

Eddie was in handcuffs along with the others. Leslie was still looking defiant, Ms. Greasy Hair was sullen and Mr. Dixon was hanging his head in resignation. I went over to Eddie to wish him good luck.

"Sorry you have to see me this way," he apologized.

"That's okay. Adam and I explained everything to the detectives, including how you helped us escape. They had no choice but to arrest you for your part in the diamond smuggling, but the younger detective said a good lawyer could have you out on bail by tomorrow. We wanted to thank you for saving our lives. Please come visit us, I know Watson would like to see you again." I reached up and kissed him on the cheek.

Adam shook one of Eddie's handcuffed hands. "That goes the same for me. Good luck."

Adam then looked at me with a mischievous grin on his face. He moved close to Mr. Dixon and pretended he was going to throw up again. Mr. Dixon jumped back so fast he almost fell over. We turned and walked away, trying not to laugh too loudly.

"You two ready to go home?" Mom asked. We both nodded our heads in full agreement. "We found your bikes and Dad has everything packed up. Now, let's get out of here."

"Wait a minute," Adam gasped. "Isn't that Vanessa and her father?"

Vanessa got out of the car and immediately the blonde dog went bounding over to her. It was Vanessa's dog that we had been chasing!

Adam's hand brushed mine as we walked over to see Vanessa.

"Do you mind?" he asked, giving my fingers a gentle squeeze.

"No," I pressed back.

Vanessa looked up and started to cry.

"Adam, I need to talk to Vanessa alone for a minute."

"Sure. I'll go help your Dad."

"Are you okay, Vanessa?"

"I'm crying because I'm happy that you found my dog, but I also just realized that Adam is your boyfriend."

"I'm sorry Vanessa, but it's been quite a day, and well, things have a funny way of turning out."

"I've known all along that you liked Adam and he liked you. Even though I've been trying real hard, Adam just wasn't interested in me except as a friend. I'll stop chasing after Adam and I hope you and I can be friends, too."

I gave her a hug. "I didn't realize until today how much I really liked Adam. He's been my best buddy for so long I hadn't thought of him being anything more than that. I guess I should thank you for helping me realize what my feelings for Adam really were."

"I'm so sorry," she said. "All I used to think about were ways to come between the two of you."

"Friends?" I said sticking out my hand.

"Friends," she replied, and we shook on it. "Can I call you later?

I'd love to hear all about how you found my precious Blondie."

"Sure, Vanessa, but not today. Right now I just want to go home and sleep."

I headed back to our car. Time to get out of here!

I looked around. "What happened to Mrs. Lee?" I asked.

"She's gone home to pack. Your father will come back tomorrow to pick her up," Mom replied. "She's agreed to stay with us for a few weeks. Mrs. Lee believes she can help you explore your Chinese heritage, and hopefully make the dreams go away." Little did we know the adventure that awaited us later that summer, searching for the *Emperor's Pendant.*

Adam and I sat quietly in the back seat of the car as Dad drove home. I reached over and took his hand.

From his usual spot on the floor, Watson opened one eye and peered up at me. I looked back at him and smiled. "Thanks again for saving us, Watson." Mom had told us that he had grabbed Dad's pant leg with his teeth and started to pull towards the marina. Seeing the jade pendant on Watson's neck made them realize that something must be wrong. When they arrived at the marina, the yacht had already left the dock, but lucky for us they could just make out its name.

I still found it hard to believe that Leslie had been so friendly with me just in case she needed Watson. The extra attention she had lavished on Watson was only to get him used to her scent. He hadn't warned us when we went onto Mr. Dixon's yacht because he knew it was Leslie hiding behind the doorway. Even after she'd knocked Adam and me unconscious, Watson was still glad to see her.

"Let that be a lesson to you, Watson. Don't go blindly giving your affections away." Watson rolled onto his back so I could rub his belly. "What a silly dog you are."

I was glad it was over and we could go back to enjoying our summer vacation. That's not to say I wouldn't do it all again, but I silently hoped that our next mystery wouldn't be quite as exciting.

THE END

ABOUT THE AUTHOR

Steve Whan lives in North Vancouver, Canada with his wife, two daughters, two dogs and two cats.

The idea for this story came to Steve after the adoption of his first daughter. Steve grew up reading the Hardy Boys. That was okay for him, but where were the novels for young girls adopted from China? Steve imagined a mystery series written for his own daughter and the tens of thousands like her. Thus Autumn Jade and her world were born.

For pictures of old Shanghai, links to useful resources and much more, please visit Autumn Jade at http://www.autumnjade.com.